"You Want A Baby, So I'll Give You A Baby,"

Griffin said evenly, making sure to hold her gaze. "I'm the guy who created your present problem, and I'll fix it."

A half laugh escaped Eva, her expression disbelieving. "Isn't it a bit much to be volunteering to fix it this way?"

"Why don't you let me worry about that part?" he responded.

"There's no spark between us."

"I disagree."

The words hung in the air between them, and he could tell she was remembering the kiss they'd shared at her apartment, just as he hadn't been able to forget it, either.

She laughed again, but it came out a trifle forced. She attempted to step around him. "Griffin, be serious—"

"I am," he said, blocking her with his arm.

She looked up at him mutely. Her lips parted.

"Why don't we kiss and put it to the test?"

Dear Reader,

Sometimes we can't see that love is nearby…until the right circumstances intrude.

I'm pleased to say this is my eighth book for the Silhouette Desire line. And with hindsight, I can see I've often played with the theme of love in surprising proximity.

Eva Tremont is determined to marry the right man. But figuring out who's right and who's wrong proves to be trickier than she imagined. As Eva discovers, behind Griffin Slater's cool, steady exterior lies a sexy, passionate man.

I hope you enjoy Eva and Griffin's story!

All my best,

Anna

ANNA DEPALO

CEO'S MARRIAGE SEDUCTION

Silhouette® Desire

Published by Silhouette Books

America's Publisher of Contemporary Romance

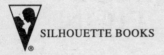

SILHOUETTE BOOKS
®

ISBN-13: 978-0-373-76859-2
ISBN-10: 0-373-76859-1

CEO'S MARRIAGE SEDUCTION

Copyright © 2008 by Anna DePalo

Visit Silhouette Books at www.eHarlequin.com

Printed in U.S.A.

Books by Anna DePalo

Silhouette Desire

Having the Tycoon's Baby #1530
Under the Tycoon's Protection #1643
Tycoon Takes Revenge #1697
Cause for Scandal #1711
Captivated by the Tycoon #1775
An Improper Affair #1803
Millionaire's Wedding Revenge #1819
CEO's Marriage Seduction #1859

ANNA DePALO

discovered she was a writer at heart when she realized most people don't walk around with a full cast of characters in their heads. She has lived in Italy and England, learned to speak French, graduated from Harvard, earned graduate degrees in political science and law, forgotten how to speak French and married her own dashing hero.

A former intellectual property attorney, Anna lives with her husband and son in New York City. Her books have consistently hit the Waldenbooks bestseller list and Nielsen BookScan's list of Top 100 bestselling romances. She has won a *Romantic Times BOOKreviews* Reviewers' Choice Award for Best First Series Romance and she's been published in over a dozen countries. Readers are invited to surf to www.desireauthors.com and can also visit Anna at www.annadepalo.com.

For Angelica Compagnone

One

"**I**'m going to marry him."

The wrong man.

No, the right man, Eva corrected herself, irritated for even momentarily adopting her father's negative perspective.

True, there was no gut feeling of *rightness,* of *destiny,* but then she told herself to stop being illogical.

How many times during her party planning career had things seemed off before proceeding without a hitch? She'd also seen what should have been perfect events erupt into flaming disasters.

No, there was no predicting the future, she decided, even as she met her father's annoyed and disbelieving gaze.

Marcus Tremont stood and slapped a hand on the massive oak desk before him. "Damn it, Eva! Are you out of your mind? Carter Newell is a fortune-hunting snake. You won't get a penny from me!"

Her lips tightened, but she refused to show how her father's words hurt. She'd come from work today—Mondays were her slow days—to meet her father in his wood-paneled library at the family estate in exclusive Mill Valley. She'd girded herself for this battle.

"Fortunately," she responded, "we don't need a penny from you. Occasions by Design is doing very well."

Her reputation in the Bay Area as a party planner had grown in the past several years. She was regularly called on by many of San Francisco's high-profile society hostesses, as well as by well-known philanthropic organizations.

Her father raked his hand through his shock of gray hair. "What you see in Carter Newell, I'll never understand."

They'd been over this ground before, each time with the same result. Somehow, though, now that her engagement was a reality, she'd hoped today would be different.

Unlike her father and his kind, *work* wasn't Carter's mistress. Instead he made *her* a priority.

"Carter loves me," she said simply.

Her father's brows snapped together. "Or your bank account."

She ground her teeth. Her father had always been wary, suspicious even, when meeting her boyfriends. She supposed it was because she was an heiress and an only child. But with Carter, the initial wariness had never eased. Of course, she'd never gotten close to the altar with any of her prior boyfriends....

"Does Carter even have a job?" her father continued. "Refresh my memory, Evangeline. What's his line of work again?"

Her father knew very well what Carter did for a living, but Eva decided to play along with his game. "Carter is an independent financial consultant."

She'd thought, the first time she'd mentioned it months ago, that Carter's profession at least would meet with her father's approval. Marcus Tremont respected getting a return on his dollar.

Instead her father's response had been lukewarm. And when she'd started hinting she was considering marrying Carter, her father's reaction had taken a sudden nosedive.

"Baloney," her father pronounced, echoing his

skepticism on previous occasions. "A trumped-up title to provide window dressing for his real occupation as an heiress hunter."

"Carter comes from money!" Despite her best intentions, they were revisiting previous arguments that had gone nowhere. She felt a headache coming on.

"He *came* from money," her father countered. "He makes a show of managing other people's money since he doesn't have any of his own."

That did it. "You're impossible! Just because the Newells aren't as wealthy as they once were, you think Carter is a fortune hunter!"

Even as she spoke, she regretted that she so frequently fell back into sounding like an adolescent when dealing with her father.

"Trust me on this, Eva. There's nothing more tenacious than a person who's trying to hold on to his economic perch in life and avoid a nasty fall."

They'd both raised their voices, and Eva gave up on trying to make the announcement of her impending marriage into a joyous occasion.

"Where's the ring?" her father asked abruptly, looking at her hand. "I don't see one."

"I don't have one yet."

Her father's expression said it all: See? What other proof do you need?

"Oh, no, you don't," she said, heading him off

before he could give voice to his thoughts. "We're picking one out *together.*"

"With what?" her father asked pointedly. "A loan from the bank?"

She supposed her engagement wouldn't really be official until she had a ring, but she refused to have the argument with her father focus on mere symbolism.

A knock sounded, calling a halt to their argument and making them both turn toward the closed library door.

"Come in," her father barked.

The door opened, and Griffin Slater strode in.

Eva's eyes narrowed.

Griffin Slater. Her father's right-hand man.

If anyone had the *perfect* credentials for a husband in her father's eyes, it was Griffin.

She disliked Griffin Slater intensely. She had since she'd met him a decade before, soon after he'd started working at Tremont Real Estate Holdings.

At first, she'd barely been aware of his existence, since he'd been just another newly minted Stanford MBA learning the ropes of the real estate business and climbing the corporate ladder.

Now thirty-five, he was more boss than employee, especially since her father's advancing age necessitated that he loosen his grip on the family real estate empire.

Griffin was also a constant reminder of her own shortcomings as her father's sole heir. She'd shown no interest in the family firm, and had instead embarked on her own business ventures right out of college at UC Berkeley.

She was well aware that her field was regarded by many as frivolous—just glorified debutante busywork. And she had no doubt Griffin Slater shared that opinion.

But at least *she'd* had the guts to build her own business rather than usurp someone else's.

Now, looking at Griffin Slater's face, she noted his expression gave nothing away. He was a master of the poker face—that is, when he wasn't baiting her.

Over six feet, he had rough chiseled features more suited to a boxer than a male model. Still, his effect on women was potent. She'd witnessed that herself at numerous social occasions over the years.

She supposed it had something to do with his piercing dark eyes. Or maybe the sable hair that insisted on curling despite being kept regimentally short. And certainly a body that was all leashed male power didn't hurt. *She'd* even given it a lingering look on more than one occasion—before she'd trapped her runaway mind.

"You're just in time for the show, Griffin," she said.

Griffin raised his eyebrows in mild interest as he shut the door behind him.

She hated the fact that her father looked relieved to see Griffin—or as she secretly liked to call him, *Mr. Fix-It*.

Now Griffin would be witness to another epic Tremont family battle. Somewhat fittingly, she thought, since he seemed to have an instinct for turning up at key moments.

"What show? I have to admit to being curious," Griffin said, his voice continuing in that mild, amused tone that never failed to irritate her.

Her father slapped his hand on his desk. "My daughter has decided to marry the most *worthless* man I know."

"Dad!" she said, outraged.

Griffin's gaze shot to her, and she felt the tension in the room shoot up.

"Who's the lucky man?"

As if he couldn't guess, Eva thought. Griffin had met Carter on a couple of occasions. Once at a casual social gathering at her parents' house, and another during a chance encounter at an art gallery opening.

Both times, Griffin had been without a date, but Eva wasn't fooled. She'd seen women come and go.

Mostly *go,* since Griffin seemed disinclined to bestow his greatness on any one woman for too long.

Her chin lifted, her eyes locking with Griffin's. Despite her father's poor introduction, there was no reason she should be defensive—she was perfectly comfortable with her decision.

"Carter Newell," she said emphatically.

Griffin strolled farther into the room. "So congratulations are in order."

She noticed he didn't say he was *offering any,* just that it was what politeness dictated—if he were being polite.

Griffin's gaze swept over her, and despite being dressed appropriately enough in a vintage Diane von Furstenberg wrap dress, she felt as if she were on display.

Her blood pressure went up. This was par for the course in her interactions with Griffin. Their conversations always had a subtext that her father was oblivious to.

"Congratulate her, but send condolences my way," her father grumbled.

Griffin's eyes focused on her hand. "Where's the ring?"

His words were such a perfect echo of Marcus Tremont's, she ground her teeth. "You're just like my father."

"And there's nothing wrong with that!" her father said.

Her eyes stayed on Griffin's, daring him to make some other comment.

Griffin's lips quirked, almost as if he was ready to diffuse the challenge that hung in the air. "You look as if you'd like to lob hors d'oeuvres at me—or maybe spear me with a dessert fork."

There it was again—an oblique, patronizing reference to her business, sailing straight over her father's head. She should have known better than to believe for a second Griffin would back away from a challenge.

She smiled thinly. "Don't tempt me."

Turning to her father, she decided to change tactics. "You know, you should be happy," she offered. "After all, the sooner I'm married, the sooner you might get the grandchild you keep referring to."

To herself, she admitted the timing of her engagement to Carter might have the teeny, tiniest thing to do with the fact that she longed for a baby.

Though she'd dated through her twenties, the right man had never come along. Her mother had entered menopause prematurely, and she didn't know how much time she herself had left. Of course, she'd taken a test, and while it indicated her egg supply wasn't dire *at the moment,* she also knew waiting was a gamble with increasingly bad odds.

She'd told Carter about her issue with premature menopause, and he'd been enthusiastic about starting a family as soon as possible after the wedding.

"Anyone but Carter Newell," her father shot back now.

She read Griffin's silence as tacit agreement with that statement. Damn him.

Her father looked from Griffin back to her, his expression grumpier than ever. "If you two were at least friendly, I could have entertained the hope you'd marry each other."

Eva sucked in a breath.

There it was, out in the open. Her father had finally given voice to what she'd always suspected he'd been thinking.

With a quick, sidelong glance, she noticed Griffin continued to look unruffled.

His reaction was so true to form, it was maddening.

She, on the other hand, was still waiting for the hot sting of embarrassment to recede from her face.

She opened her mouth.

"Marcus," Griffin drawled before she could speak, "you know Eva is too—"

If he said *frivolous,* she swore she'd kick him in the shins.

"—hot-tempered for me."

She clamped her mouth shut. How could she argue when she'd just been thinking of clobbering him?

Griffin's eyes mocked her, as if he knew what she'd been contemplating.

She swung her attention back to her father.

She sometimes felt like just another prized possession in Marcus Tremont's asset portfolio—and by marrying Carter Newell, she supposed her father wasn't getting the return he'd banked on.

Still, she refused to weaken. "Mom and I will be checking out possible venues and going dress shopping."

Her father's eyebrows lowered. "Your mother knows about this already?"

She pasted on a sunny smile. "I suggested that's what my plans were to her before I came in here, yes. But I decided to go beard the lion in his den by myself."

Her father glowered.

"I hope to see you at the wedding—whether you can bring yourself to give me away or not." The words were said flippantly, but a thread of emotion ran beneath them that she refused to analyze too closely.

She turned on her heel and, not sparing another glance at Griffin, strode out of her father's library.

She was everything he desired, but in the wrong package.

Griffin watched Eva Tremont sashay out of the library, her clingy knit dress hugging every curve.

His lips twisted.

She was quite a package, and had been ever since he'd first laid eyes on her. She was equal parts head-strong heiress, savvy businesswoman and sexy single woman.

It was also clear she despised him. If he had to guess, he'd say it was because he reminded her of every way she fell short as Marcus Tremont's heir.

That he'd more recently become CEO of Tremont REH was probably just rubbing salt in the wounds.

Still, his ties to Marcus Tremont and Tremont REH were also the reason Eva was off-limits to him, he reminded himself. He wasn't the commitment type, and *committed* was the only type of relationship that would be acceptable with the boss's daughter.

Of course, now that he remained on as CEO of Tremont REH more as a favor to Marcus than anything else, Eva wasn't really the boss's daughter any longer, but she remained related to someone he valued as a friend, a colleague and a mentor.

"That bastard Newell," Marcus Tremont said, calling him back from his thoughts.

Griffin had met Carter Newell only a couple of times. But he'd been able to size the guy up as a smooth operator on the make.

When Carter had trumpeted his skills as a financial advisor, Griffin had listened detachedly, unimpressed by the guy's salesmanship—not to mention that he was happy with his stockbroker and liked to keep an eye on the markets himself.

And yet, despite the sales pitch, he'd gotten the impression Carter didn't like him much, judging by the sour expression that had flitted across the guy's face from time to time.

Carter had obviously done some sizing up of his own and come to a conclusion he didn't like: Griffin was Marcus Tremont's anointed successor. His possible future father-in-law's *single, unattached* successor.

Without a doubt, Newell had put him down as a rival for control of the money spout, and possibly for Eva as well.

Evidently, though, Carter had been willing to put personal feelings aside where financial gain was concerned—namely, reeling in another client.

And *that's* what bothered him, Griffin thought. Not just for himself, but for Eva. If Carter was willing to overlook a lot to score another client, how much would he be willing to do to acquire a rich wife?

Griffin watched as Marcus Tremont's eyes met his. "Look into it for me."

He tensed. "What are you asking?"

He had a good idea, but he didn't want there to be any room for misunderstanding.

Marcus gestured dismissively. "I mean, find out what you can about Carter Newell. Get the investigator that we use for Tremont REH." The older man's look turned grim. "I want to know what Carter Newell is hiding *before* he becomes my son-in-law."

Griffin lifted his eyebrows but was careful to keep his expression in place otherwise. "You have reason to believe he's hiding something?"

Marcus regarded him steadily. "What I know about the Newells, I don't like. They were able to hide their decline in wealth for a long time. Subterfuge is the family currency."

"I see. Still, if Eva found out…"

He let the thought trail off. He just wanted to make sure the older man appreciated the possible consequences of his decision. Marcus might do irreparable damage to his relationship with his daughter if Eva discovered they'd had Carter investigated.

And as far as his own relationship with Eva went, well, that was bound to head further south.

"There's no reason for Eva to know," Marcus said brusquely, his eyes sharpening. "Unless of course, we pin something on Newell—in which case, it'll be well worth the price to save her from that slick salesman."

Griffin nodded.

The truth was he'd derive some pleasure in bringing down Carter Newell if the guy wasn't on the up-and-up.

He pushed aside the thought that the cost *to himself* of having Carter investigated might be too high....

Two

Griffin stared out the window of his Pacific Heights mansion at the twinkling evening lights of San Francisco Bay. His grip on his wineglass constricted, putting dangerous pressure on the delicate crystal, as he thought back over the events of earlier that day.

Though he'd agreed to it, Marcus's request had put him in a difficult position.

Over the years, he'd put his own selfish desires aside where Eva was concerned. Still, he'd fantasized about making love to her on numerous occasions—even though she irritated and perplexed him by turns.

She reminded him of a sleek, lithe cat. Everything was perfectly proportioned, and exercise kept her body limber and supple.

Her straight black hair hung in a curtain past her shoulders in a blunt cut. Her mouth was a little too large for her face, and her topaz eyes tilted upward at the corners. And yet, those elements added character instead of suggesting she fell short of ideal beauty.

Now he was being asked to dig up dirt on the man that she intended to marry—the man, his lips curled tightly, she fancied herself in love with.

But he couldn't say no to Marcus Tremont's request. Because, all else aside, Griffin found himself agreeing with Marcus's instincts where Carter Newell was concerned.

Not to mention he owed Marcus a debt that couldn't be repaid.

After his parents' death in a private plane crash when he'd just gotten out of high school, he'd become guardian to his fifteen-year-old brother, Josh, and fourteen-year-old sister, Monica. He'd had to become an adult almost overnight and had become grimly determined to succeed on his own in the world.

Fortunately, though his parents had not left behind a lavish estate, it had been significant enough to allow him to send his younger siblings to boarding school and to further his own education.

After college and business school, he'd been given a break by Marcus, a business acquaintance of his father's, in the form of a job with Tremont REH, where he could learn the ropes of the real estate business.

The business relationship had proven lucrative to them both. Griffin had soon discovered he had the Midas touch when it came to real estate deals. He'd eventually formed his own company, Evkit Investments, and become immensely wealthy through savvy management of his own ever-expanding real estate portfolio.

But loyalty to Marcus Tremont had kept him involved with Tremont REH. When Marcus had decided two years ago it was time to step back from the day-to-day management of Tremont REH, he'd asked Griffin to take over the reins as CEO. Marcus had insisted that, in his continuing position as chairman of the board, there was no one he trusted more at the helm of the company he'd spent a lifetime building.

The two companies had merged their office space when Griffin had become CEO of both. And since Evkit Investments and Tremont REH pursued different business interests, there'd been no issue of competition between the companies. By Griffin's deliberate design, Evkit had acquired residential real estate rather than become a player in commercial office space.

Griffin wouldn't betray Marcus by competing with Tremont REH.

He paused now, his mind turning back to Eva.

As much as he wanted her, he didn't understand her. She exasperated him with her blithe lack of interest in Tremont REH. As a family member, she had a position on the company's board of directors, but that was the extent of her involvement.

He, on the other hand, could appreciate firsthand what Marcus had built. He'd spent years creating a company to match—and by many measures, exceed—Tremont REH's reputation. He'd also put time and effort toward growing Tremont REH, especially since he'd become CEO.

Griffin stared unseeingly at San Francisco's lights.

Still, he couldn't escape the fact that, against all reason, he remained attracted to Eva. When he was around her, he got an adrenaline rush—a heady sensation that had him feeling as if he were drunk on euphoria.

She challenged him, and he thrived on challenges.

He'd never acted on the attraction because he couldn't sleep with Marcus Tremont's daughter without there being…consequences. And Eva's obvious dislike for him made it easy to walk the line.

He'd also already had enough commitment to last a lifetime. He certainly wasn't looking to jump into another to, say, *a wife*.

He'd been *committed* to raising his younger siblings and *committed* to making sure they found their paths in the world.

It was only in the last couple of years, in fact, that he felt as if he could exhale. His brother, Josh, had finished his medical residency and become a surgeon in Denver, where he'd recently married his college sweetheart, Tessa.

Likewise, his sister, Monica, the head of a school for learning disabled children, had gotten married two years ago to a film producer, Ben Corrigan, and was settled in L.A. She was expecting her first child in five months.

He was proud of his siblings, and relieved they'd become well-adjusted adults who'd found their personal happiness.

His job was finally done.

He wasn't taking on responsibility for anyone else.

Still, the thought of Eva throwing herself away on a loser like Carter Newell made him want to put a hole in the wall.

If he couldn't have her, he damned well wasn't going to let her waste herself on a gamesman like Newell. Even if he knew that if Eva ever found out he'd done her father's dirty work, he could kiss goodbye to any minimally civilized relationship they continued to have.

With that thought, he grimly reached for his cell phone. He had Ron Winslow's number programmed in.

From time to time, he'd used the private investigator to smoke out the truth about potential real estate investments.

When Ron picked up, they exchanged brief greetings.

After a moment, Griffin cut to the chase. "I've got a new assignment for you."

"He's impossible."

"He's your father."

Eva sighed. She'd left her parents' estate earlier that day, right after the conversation with her father, and retreated to her town house condo in San Francisco's Russian Hill neighborhood.

Now she sat, curled up on her couch with her cell phone, talking to her mother, who'd called to make sure everything was okay.

"I was hoping for the best."

"He'll come around."

Eva silently disagreed with her mother's assessment. She knew just how stubborn her father could be—and during moments when she was being honest with herself, she could admit she'd inherited his stubbornness.

"The more important question," her mother continued, "is whether *you're* sure you want to marry Carter—"

"Of course!" Her reply was quick and snappy. She was still smarting from the confrontation with her father—in Griffin Slater's presence, of all people.

"Because there's no rush," her mother persisted. "The test showed you have time."

"Yes, but how much?" she replied automatically.

She'd told her mother that she'd gone in for a test to gauge the quality of her egg supply. Now she wondered from her mother's concerned tone whether she'd appeared too preoccupied with her biological clock.

"Eva—"

"Mom."

Her mother sighed.

"What do you think of Carter?" Eva blurted, and then could have kicked herself.

"I just want you to be happy."

"I want to marry Carter. I do," she said, adopting her most reassuring voice—the one she used to sooth jittery clients before a big bash.

A beep sounded on her cell phone, followed by another.

"Mom, I have another call coming in."

She checked the screen and realized it was her friend Beth Harding. She was deep into planning with Beth for a party the Hardings would be throwing at their mansion in a couple of weeks.

"It's Beth," she said to her mother.

"Okay, sweetie. I'll let you go. We'll talk another time about picking a wedding venue so you can set a date."

She felt her spirits lift. At least her mother was willing to go into cheerful wedding mode.

"Thanks, Mom," she said, before switching over to the incoming call.

"Hi, Beth," she said. "I've found some great Art Deco props for the party. It's a company that supplies movie sets down in L.A."

Beth and her husband, Oliver, would be hosting a party in a couple of weeks at their Palo Alto estate to benefit San Francisco–area children's hospitals.

She and Beth had decided that a 1930s theme would be a nice surprise for Beth's octogenarian grandmother, who lived in a guesthouse on Beth's estate and who was still spry enough to hit a dance floor.

Beth laughed. "Wonderful."

"I've rented some fantastic mohair club chairs, a couple of burled wood wet bars and several frosted glass lighting pieces. And I found these ideal cobalt mirrored serving trays!"

"It all sounds great, but the party isn't the reason I was calling."

Eva slumped. "Let me guess."

"Oh, come on. Don't hold out on me."

She'd filled in Beth on the fact that she and Carter were going to pick out a ring, and that she was making one last attempt to sway her father.

She pressed a hand to her forehead. "Where do I begin? The *bad* or the *worse?*"

"Oh, come on. It wasn't that terrible!"

Beth had an unswerving sunny outlook. "Oh, come on" happened to be one of her favorite sayings.

"It was bad," Eva replied ominously. "Let's see, the *bad* was that my father went postal. The *worse* was that Griffin Slater happened to be around to witness it."

Beth sucked in a breath. "Oh, no!"

"Oh, yes."

She filled in Beth about the details of the confrontation in her father's study, and Beth made sympathetic noises at regular intervals.

"I hope I never see Griffin Slater again," she

declared when she finished the sorry story, though she knew it was a vain hope.

"Umm…"

Beth's tone made her suddenly wary. "Tell me you didn't invite him to your party?"

"Eva, I had to! He and Oliver have known each other for years."

She groaned. She and Beth had picked out the invitation together, but Beth had submitted her final guest list directly to the printer.

"Just my luck," she grumbled.

"He may not come," Beth pointed out.

"If he knows I'm planning it, he probably won't," she responded, the thought brightening her mood.

Griffin never showed at her parties. It was one of the reasons she'd concluded he was dismissive of her business.

"Have you thought about your costume?" Beth asked, obviously trying to change the subject.

"At the moment," she said dryly, "I'm thinking that appearing with Carter as Nick & Nora would be appropriate."

Beth laughed.

She'd been only half joking, Eva thought to herself. Appearing as the Dashiell Hammett sleuths—a retired detective and his wealthy socialite wife whose family believes she married beneath herself—would definitely ring true at the moment.

"Remind me to dig out my Nick & Nora cosmetics case for you then," Beth said. "Whoever thought to create a women's brand out of those characters had a stroke of genius."

"Thanks," she deadpanned.

After she ended her call with Beth, she sat back against her couch and closed her eyes.

Despite herself, she kept replaying the awful moment when her father had come out and said he'd entertained hopes of her marrying Griffin.

Griffin as her husband?

As if.

Yes, she felt the energy whenever Griffin entered a room, but only because he knew how to press her buttons, damn it.

"I've got some bombshell news."

Griffin's hand tightened on the phone.

It had been over two weeks since his call with Ron Winslow, but now the sound of the private investigator's voice at the other end of the line brought his mind back to Eva.

As if he hadn't been thinking about her enough already.

"What have you got?" he said evenly, swiveling

his mesh chair away from his desk and toward the panel of floor-to-ceiling windows behind him.

His office at Tremont REH sat high above the bustle of San Francisco's Union Square.

Ron cleared his throat. "Newell is an operator all right—"

"I figured."

"—but not in the way you're thinking."

He tensed. "What do you mean?"

"I mean Romeo is two-timing his Juliet."

Griffin cursed under his breath. He hadn't been expecting this kind of dirt to be sticking to Newell.

"You've always delivered the goods, Ron, but I've got to ask—are you sure?"

This was, after all, Marcus Tremont's daughter they were talking about. She moved in rarified social circles. If Eva's scummy would-be fiancé was cheating on her, they were dealing with news that would eventually make the rounds of San Francisco society.

"I'm messengering the evidence to you as we speak," Ron responded. "There's a video, shots taken with the telephoto lens and even—" Ron chuckled without humor "—an audio recording. What you choose to do with this hot potato is your business."

Griffin knew without asking what Ron meant.

It would be up to him to decide what evidence to share with whom.

He didn't relish the thought of disclosing Newell's philandering to Eva. Especially since all he could think about was rearranging Carter's elegant face.

"How did you discover Newell is seeing another woman?" he asked.

"Fell into my lap," Ron replied. "I was tailing him, wondering whether I'd come up with anything interesting. A few days in, I followed him to a restaurant in Berkeley. Turned out he was there to rendezvous with a Jessica Alba look-alike."

The bastard.

Griffin wondered whether Newell had a type. Eva didn't fit as a Jessica Alba look-alike. She was more a Rose McGowan or Katharine McPhee.

And maybe, tellingly, he realized, that was the point. Eva wasn't Carter's type. The guy was only attracted to her money.

"While Newell and the woman sat at the restaurant bar," Ron went on, "I greased the palm of one of the waiters to find out which table they'd reserved. I was able to slip a microphone onto the wall next to their seats before they sat down, and I laid claim to the next table."

The investigator added with a snort, "You won't believe the crap I've got on tape."

Oh, he could believe it all right, Griffin thought cynically, picturing smooth-as-cream Carter in his mind. The problem was going to be explaining it all to Eva.

"Afterward, I got them pulling into a dim parking lot behind a nondescript office building," Ron continued with dark relish. "Newell's not even shelling out for a cheap motel on a regular basis."

"Great."

Not great. Ron's information made him wonder just how empty Newell's pockets were and how desperate Carter was to marry an heiress.

"I've got the video and telephoto lens for the parking lot interlude."

"Are you sure this wasn't a one-night stand?" Griffin asked.

He wanted to go to Eva with an airtight case if he had to rip rose-colored glasses from her eyes. He didn't want Newell to be able to argue he'd just had a lapse in judgment.

"Not to worry, I got them on other occasions," Ron responded. "They had a tryst at a motel two days ago."

"Damn it."

"I've also got evidence our man Carter has no significant assets and is living on credit to fund his lifestyle," Ron said offhandedly. "In fact, he may be just about all tapped out."

Griffin at last let himself acknowledge they'd hit the mother lode with Newell. It made him want to wring the guy's neck.

And as much as he knew that Eva needed to comprehend Carter was a two-timing snake, he didn't want her to be hurt.

He raked his fingers through his hair, his mind working. "Ron, I'd appreciate it if you didn't say anything to anyone, including Marcus, about what you've uncovered."

"Will do."

"I'll look for your package," he said grimly before ending the call.

When Ron's box arrived an hour later—just in time to be served up with lunch for his delectation—he told his secretary to hold his calls.

Griffin set the cardboard box on his desk and sliced it open with an envelope opener he kept in a desk drawer. He pulled out a financial profile, an envelope marked Photos, an audio CD and a DVD.

He surveyed the evidence with distaste. This was the material that could set Eva's life on a different trajectory. Yet it looked harmless enough unless you were asking it to give up its secrets.

He flipped through the stapled sheets that constituted Ron's financial dossier on Carter. The report was just as Ron had described. Carter had a mortgaged apartment in San Francisco and sizable loans at the bank. He was no Bill Gates, and probably not even in the ballpark of his Newell antecedents.

Griffin opened the envelope next. A dozen or so photos fell out, and he spread them out on the desk in front of him.

There were a couple of shots of a man who looked like Carter Newell in a parking lot, embracing and kissing a stacked brunette.

Another photo showed the couple walking hand in hand into a restaurant. From their body language, and the way the woman leaned close to the man next to her, it was clear the two were more than friends.

Griffin guessed these photos were taken when Ron had tailed Newell to the restaurant in Berkeley.

Griffin focused on the remaining photos. They looked like they'd been taken at another point when Ron had caught up with the pair. They showed the couple meeting in a park, embracing under a tree near a walking path, and then kissing and touching on a park bench.

The photos were decent evidence as far as they went. But they weren't strong proof Carter and the woman had progressed to being lovers.

Griffin sat behind his desk and popped the DVD into his computer. Then he leaned back in his chair to watch.

The video began just as Ron had described.

A car was parked in a deserted lot illuminated by yellow streetlights. After a few moments, it began to shake and move with the exertions of its occupants. Eventually a disheveled Carter and a half-dressed woman emerged, and Carter helped the woman with the clasp of her bra and her sweater. While the woman brushed her hair and applied lipstick, Carter ran his hands over her. Finally the pair made it back into the car and drove off.

A second segment on the DVD showed Carter and the brunette arriving at a motel. Through the glass window of the motel's front office, Carter and his female companion could be seen checking in. Afterward, the pair headed to a second-floor room.

When the video ended, Griffin leaned down to pop the DVD out of the computer.

His lips twisted. Apparently Carter wasn't too cheap to shell out for a bed *occasionally.* Or maybe in some situations his sexual encounters didn't need to be so hurried because he didn't have to run back to Eva.

The bastard.

Griffin switched out the DVD for the CD Ron had sent, set it to Play and leaned back in his chair again.

After a few seconds, the audio came on. A man

and woman could be heard conversing against a low murmur of background noise and voices.

At first the couple talked about banal things like the menu, but after a waiter had departed with their order, the conversation turned sexual.

The woman used Carter's name a couple of times, while he referred to her as "Sondra" or, more often, "baby."

Griffin rolled his eyes as the woman recalled her last sexual encounter with Carter, then pouted about not having more of his time.

Yeah, right, Griffin thought. If Carter wasn't set on reeling in an heiress, he supposed the woman had a fighting chance of getting more of Carter's attention.

Griffin listened as Carter tried to placate his companion with assurances that he'd soon whisk her away for a Mexican vacation and that he was expecting a windfall that he couldn't go into details about.

Griffin felt his temper ignite. It was clear Carter's *windfall* was his upcoming marriage. Obviously Carter wasn't going to divulge to his lover that he was two-timing an heiress. It might expose him to blackmail.

Carter was toast, Griffin thought. If he ever got his hands on pedigree boy…

The audio recording continued to follow the couple through their meal. Toward the end of it,

Carter began to describe in intimate detail what he wanted to do to Sondra.

When the audio recording ended, Griffin mulled over his options and didn't like any of them.

Just how the hell was he supposed to share this with Eva? She'd hate him for life, if she didn't despise him already.

Later that day, he had the misfortune of running into Marcus when the older man stopped by his office just as he was about to exit it.

"Have you heard anything yet from Ron?" Marcus asked.

"Nothing," Griffin heard himself respond.

He didn't even have to think about his reply.

But it occurred to him afterward it was the first time he'd had to lie to Marcus Tremont about anything important.

Three

Eva curled up on the couch. Her Bluetooth headset allowed her to speak with her mother while she paged through one of several magazines about San Francisco's social scene. She liked to keep up with what her clients, as well as her business competition, were doing.

It was a Tuesday evening—a night of the week she could usually count on to be able to kick back and relax.

As a party planner, she lived on the opposite timetable from the rest of the world. Midweek was her weekend, while at the end of the week, she became turbocharged as things heated up at work. On weekends, she was often supervising her employees at some museum fund-raiser or at a social-ite-hosted charity lunch, making sure everything went off flawlessly.

Now, however, her midweek was being consumed by wedding planning.

"What about the Fairmont?" her mother asked.

"I'm not sure it's *exactly* what I'm looking for...."

It had quickly become apparent to her that her mother was picturing a wedding for hundreds of family, friends and assorted business associates.

The historic Fairmont Hotel, with its gilded rooms projecting an old-world elegance, was well suited for the purpose.

The problem was, Eva acknowledged, that she herself longed for something more intimate.

But Carter seemed to be on the same page as her mother.

"What about the Palace of Fine Arts then?" her mother asked, naming another popular and elegant San Francisco wedding location.

Eva sighed.

"I heard that," her mother said.

"Did you?" she asked absently.

"It's too bad your father owns only commercial

office space," her mother remarked with dry humor. "At a time like this, we could use an inside edge."

"I'm not sure Dad will even attend the wedding."

"Oh, he'll come around," her mother said breezily, repeating her unwavering opinion up to now. "You're his only child, and though he may have a hard time showing it sometimes, he really does care about you."

The buzzer sounded, and Eva wondered who could be ringing her doorbell.

Her town house condo was in a low-rise development in Russian Hill. Though she had friends nearby, no one was in the habit of dropping by unannounced. And she knew her close friend, Beth Harding, was out of town at the moment.

"Mom," she said, "I've got to go. Someone's at the door."

"All right. I'll give you a ring tomorrow so we can continue to talk about wedding plans."

Her heart lightened. "It'll be fun."

This was what she'd looked forward to. Sharing one of life's passages with her mother.

"Oh, I just know I'm going to get teary seeing you in a wedding gown," her mother responded, her voice suddenly choked.

Eva felt tears clog her own throat. "I know, Mom. I know."

After ending the call with her mother, she slipped her feet into her shoes and went to her front door.

Because the ground level of her condo housed a garage and storage area, her front door was one flight up from the street, accessible via an enclosed external stairwell, at the foot of which was a tall locked iron gate.

She opened the door and locked eyes with the last person she expected to see darkening her doorstep. *Griffin Slater.*

Automatically she tensed.

"Can I come up?" he called.

Her mind ran over the possibilities. *Yes, no, when hell freezes over?*

"What are you doing here?" she asked, her tone coming out more suspicious than she intended.

He seemed to find her question amusing.

"Would you believe I just happened to be in the neighborhood?" he responded.

"Actually, no," she replied, even as good manners impelled her down the stairs to open the gate.

She knew he lived in nearby Pacific Heights, but she'd *never* run into him on her home turf.

They ran in different circles. She was too bohemian, too much of a free spirit, she was sure, for Griffin Slater's taste. On the other hand, he probably even scheduled sex with the women he dated.

She didn't understand why he was so irritating by nature. His siblings were pleasant people. She even counted his sister among her extended circle of friends.

With Griffin, however, she couldn't shake the feeling she was letting the Big Bad Wolf in.

As usual, he wore a conservative business suit—this time set off by a herringbone shirt and bright yellow-and-blue striped tie. In contrast, her mauve shirt and tan pants—which she'd worn at work that day and hadn't yet changed out of—felt almost casual in comparison.

Opening the gate, her eyes met his, her one step advantage on the stairs bringing her close to his height.

The corner of his mouth lifted. "Am I invited in?"

"Are you on a mission for my father?" she countered, her eyes skimming over the envelope in his hand. "If so—"

"Mission impossible," he said. "I know."

She gave him a serene smile. Well, at least they both knew where they stood.

"Actually I'm here for a personal reason."

Despite herself, she was intrigued. She didn't think she and Griffin had anything of a personal nature to say to each other, but curiosity got the better of her.

She turned, leaving him to follow her up the stairs. "Come on in."

On the way up, she could *feel* his presence behind her. Why, oh why, did she always have to be so aware of him?

When they stepped inside her condo, she shut the front door. "Can I get you something?"

"Nothing, thanks," he replied.

She watched him look around her apartment, which was almost loftlike in its layout. From the marble-floored entry area, the cool ambiance of the living and dining room area was visible. The kitchen, with its granite surfaces and stainless steel appliances, was situated beyond a waist-high counter with bar stools.

She watched Griffin's eyes linger on the display of fresh flowers set on a tabletop. She loved newly cut blooms.

Still, since she was a little unnerved by his presence in her apartment, she was grateful no more personal touches were visible. Her bedroom—along with a guest room, two baths and a terrace—was tucked away upstairs.

She wondered again about why he was here. "Is it Dad?" she blurted. "Is something wrong with my father?"

Griffin had said her father hadn't requested he

come, but that didn't mean Griffin's appearance at her door didn't involve her father.

Her father was in his late sixties, and she dreaded the day something would befall him. As strained as their relationship sometimes was, she still loved him. And she worried he would try to protect her by hiding any health problems until they were dire.

"No, don't worry," Griffin responded. Then he asked abruptly, "Do you know what Carter was doing two nights ago?"

Caught off guard, she said, "No. Why?"

Griffin regarded her intently, and even though not a muscle moved in his face, there was something she didn't like in his expression.

A sense of unease settled in the pit of her stomach.

"Why?" she repeated.

Griffin's eyes pinned her like lasers. "Carter Newell has been sleeping with another woman behind your back. He was with her two nights ago."

She looked at him uncomprehendingly, but after a moment, his words hit her, washing over her like one big tidal wave of disaster.

Her mouth worked.

She was still unable to look away from Griffin's eyes, and somehow they were the only thing keeping her standing.

Panicky dread coursed through her, making her feel ill.

"How—how do you know this?" she managed at last, showing a composure she didn't feel.

"Does it matter?" he asked, shoving his hands in his pockets.

Because he'd seemed ready for the question, she became suspicious.

"How did you find out?" she asked, trying again, her tone sharpening. "You and Carter don't run in the same circles."

Griffin shrugged.

"My father put you up to this, didn't he?" she accused.

When he continued to look at her implacably, she said, "Answer the question, Griffin. You're a hired gun, aren't you?"

Griffin's jaw worked. "Your father started the ball rolling by asking me to look into it, yes."

"You mean he asked you to have Carter investigated," she responded. "Let's not sugarcoat it, shall we? He asked you to sic Tremont REH's usual investigator on him, right?"

It was an interrogation, and from the look on Griffin's face, he didn't like it one bit.

Too bad, she thought. Since he'd *volunteered* to be the messenger, he'd asked for it.

"Does it matter how I found out?" Griffin asked.

"Did you tell my father you were coming here?"

He looked at her, his face carved in granite. "I didn't tell your father anything—including what the investigator found out. I thought you should know first."

"Misplaced gallantry, Griffin?" she said mockingly.

His face tightened. "I thought you'd appreciate it."

She glared at him. "*Appreciate it?* Appreciate you've had my fiancé investigated? Appreciate you've acted at my father's bidding?"

His eyes narrowed.

"Oh, I *appreciate* it. I just don't know which of you to thank first. Carter, my father or *you.*"

"Aren't you sidestepping the real issue?"

"What if I said I don't believe you?"

His expression chided her. "You know the investigator has evidence to back me up."

For the first time, she focused on the envelope in his hand. "Let me see it."

She moved to take the envelope from him.

"No."

She came to a stop. *"No?"*

"I'll let you see *some* of it. I brought some photos—and evidence that Carter has barely got a cent to his name."

He said no more, but she understood the implications. If Carter had no money, and on top of it all, was cheating on her, all signs pointed to *one* reason why he'd been willing to marry *her.*

She hated coming to the conclusion her father had been right. Sure Carter had floated the idea of a prenuptial agreement, but he'd looked relieved when she—silly, romantic soul—had put the kibosh on the idea. And prenup or no prenup, Carter would have enjoyed the lifestyle to which her income and her trust fund would have made him accustomed.

As if that weren't enough, for the second time, she felt like the recipient of Griffin's misplaced gallantry. He was trying to spare her from seeing the sordid proof of Carter's betrayal.

"Trying to protect me, Griffin?" she challenged. "Don't you think it's a little late for that?"

His expression closed. "You don't act like a woman who's just found out the man she loves has been two-timing her."

"Are you questioning the strength of my feelings for Carter?"

He just looked at her coolly.

"You really are a piece of work, you know that?" she said. "First, you have my fiancé investigated, then you question my feelings. Do you always rub salt in the wounds?"

"Just noting the facts."

"Did you expect me to break down and weep in front of you?" she tossed back at him.

"I suppose the tears will flow when you're done being angry."

That did it. She stalked forward to grab the envelope from him, but he was too fast for her.

He held the envelope aloft, and she wound up knocking against him instead of seizing the photos.

She jumped up, once, twice, but he was bigger, taller and stronger.

"Damn you!" she said between gritted teeth, tears stinging her eyes. Was she destined to be thwarted by all the men in her life?

"I'm *damned* all right," he responded in a clipped tone.

"You've never experienced the sting of rejection, have you? *Noooo,* of course not. You're Mr. Oh-So-Perfect. *Mr. Fix-It.*"

"You don't know the first thing about it."

"Oh, right, I forget," she quavered, swiping at a tear. "You're a *man.* You don't need to worry about your biological clock ticking, about the fact your mother entered menopause prematurely, about the fact you're past thirty and closing in on thirty-five and the bell may toll on your fertility before you're ready for it."

While she was giving him a piece of her mind,

she realized he'd gone still as a rock, his expression frozen.

"I'll *never* have a baby now."

And then mortifyingly, the tears welled up and burst from her.

Griffin tossed the envelope aside, and grasped her by the arms as sobs racked her.

His mouth came down on hers, as he pressed her back against the wall behind her.

Stunned, she went still.

He plundered her mouth, and she was swamped by the sensation of him. His hard, lean body pushed against her, and she picked up the scent of Ivory soap that clung to his skin.

Then as anger and frustration poured out of her, she kissed him back.

It was a brutal kiss, a contest of wills. She made sounds halfway between moans of pleasure and groans of angry frustration.

Griffin had infiltrated her house, stripping her of every protective layer and exposing her vulnerability, and then had the nerve to kiss her.

She tried to shrug off his grasp, but he just pinned her with his body, his hand coming up to hold her head still.

His hot mouth devoured her, and sizzling sensation skated across her skin.

Finally, however, she pulled together the frayed ends of rationality and tore her mouth from his.

She shoved at him, and he rocked back on his heels.

Her sobs had faded away, and anger now completely filled the void. Whatever she'd felt toward her father and Carter, it was directed all at Griffin for the moment.

Confused and disturbed by his kiss, she grasped at the first thing she could think of to lash out at him with.

"Did you think I'd be ripe for the picking now that Carter's proved faithless?" she asked, trembling. "That I'd be so desperate…"

She left the sentence unfinished. *So desperate she'd even consider taking up with him.*

Griffin's expression closed. "Trust me," he ground out. "The last way I'd describe you is *desperate.*"

Then, before she could say anything else, he turned and strode to the door, letting it slam shut behind him.

She dashed to her front window and watched as he emerged from her house seconds later and climbed into his Porsche convertible.

She lingered to watch as he pulled away down the street.

Only then did she become aware of the fact that she had two fingers pressed to her lips—where she could still feel his kiss.

Four

Eva already had plans to meet Carter for dinner the following night.

She breezed into The Last Supper Club at a quarter past seven. If she had her way, she thought, this would be *Carter's* last supper.

She was dressed in a Proenza Schouler little black dress. Her *kiss-off* dress, she liked to think of it as now.

She'd called ahead to the restaurant so the staff could advise Carter when he arrived that she would be a little late.

Now, she found Carter exactly where she expected him. He was already seated, enjoying a glass of red wine and perusing the menu.

His face brightened when he spotted her. "Eva! Glad you're here."

He wouldn't be glad for long, Eva thought.

She stopped when she reached his table, not bothering to take a seat.

Carter rose, and Eva watched the gesture cynically.

When she'd first met Carter, she'd been taken by his gentlemanly manners, but now she saw them as just another piece of artifice in his carefully constructed facade.

Her gaze moved over him.

He was wearing an off-white linen blazer over an open-collar light blue shirt that accentuated the paleness of his eyes. His dirty-blond hair was artfully mussed.

His appearance struck her now as *too perfect,* and Eva called herself a fool for the thousandth time in the last twenty-four hours.

She thought about Carter's willingness to have kids right away, and wondered now whether his enthusiasm had been feigned. On the other hand, kids would have solidified his claim on her money.

Even Carter's push for a big wedding appeared suspect in retrospect. A large wedding would have been a major networking opportunity for him since the cream of San Francisco society would have been in attendance.

Carter reached to pull out her chair, but she continued to stand where she was.

Belatedly, Carter took in her expression and frowned.

"Is something wrong?" he asked.

"Tell me one thing," she said bluntly. "Is it true?"

"Is what true?"

"Are you seeing another woman?"

Carter's expression momentarily registered shock, and then went blank.

Oh, he was good, she thought.

"I don't know what you mean," he responded carefully, and then his face softened. "Eva, I'm *engaged* to *you.*"

He reached for her, but she sidestepped him. She'd been expecting delay and obfuscation.

She pulled the photos from the outer pocket of her purse and tossed them on the table. She watched as he scanned them.

Carter's face first showed puzzlement, then shock and, finally, a subtle tightening of the muscles.

When Carter looked up at her, however, she realized he still wasn't willing to give up the game.

His expression was arranged in lines that were relaxed and reassuring.

"Eva, I can explain—"

"There's more," she said, cutting him off.

After Griffin had left her apartment yesterday, she'd retrieved the photos he'd left behind. She'd spread them out on her coffee table and stared at them until her mind was numb. They'd been incriminating enough—showing Carter dallying with a busty brunette—that she'd wondered what Griffin *wasn't* letting her see. A videotape, perhaps?

Now, her eyes bore into Carter's, and after several moments, she watched as his shoulders lowered.

"Who gave you these?" he demanded.

"Does it matter?" she retorted.

She knew she sounded just like Griffin had yesterday—dismissing the importance of the photos' origin—but she didn't care.

"Your father," Carter guessed.

"Griffin Slater," she shot back.

She took some satisfaction in contradicting him. Technically it had been Griffin who had handed her the photos.

Carter's brows snapped together. "The guy I met at a gathering at your parents' estate a few months ago? The CEO of Tremont REH?"

She nodded.

"Acting at your father's request, I'll bet," Carter guessed again.

She said nothing, but her hands fisted at her sides.

After a moment, Carter's lips quirked up in dry amusement. "Your father always hated me," he said almost ruefully. "He had it in for me from the beginning,"

"That's it? That's all you have to say?"

Carter's expression cooled. "What do you want me to say, Eva?"

"You were taking me for a ride! You lied to me— cheated on me!" she flung at him. "Were you planning to carry on with her right through the wedding and honeymoon?"

Carter glanced around them. "Eva, you're creating a scene."

"I don't give a damn!"

"This isn't the place to be having this discussion."

"I can't think of a better one, actually," she retorted before coming to the point. "Why were you marrying me, Carter?"

He didn't respond for a moment. Then his eyes took on a calculated edge. "What about your motives for marrying me? *A baby.*"

"I was up-front about my reproductive issues, Carter," she snapped. "It hardly amounts to a betrayal of trust."

She'd thought she'd been marrying Carter for all the right reasons. She hadn't just wanted a baby. *Had she?*

"And that was some ride you were taking me on where Griffin Slater was concerned."

"What?"

Carter raised his eyebrows. "Don't ask me to believe there's nothing between you and Mr. CEO. A guy doesn't step up to the plate with evidence like this without a damned good reason. I saw the way he watched you at your parents' party."

Her eyes widened.

Unbelievable. Carter was turning the tables on her, making it seem as if *she* was the one who had to defend herself.

"Even if Griffin Slater was a hired gun," Carter continued, "he could have just forked over the incriminating evidence to your father instead of going to console the devastated heiress himself."

Carter's tone was mocking, and her father's words reverberated through her mind.

Heiress hunter.

She suddenly saw that Carter was like a penny dipped in acid. *Fool's gold.*

And then she did the one thing guaranteed to dull the penny.

"Oh, I wouldn't say *devastated* is the right word."

She grabbed the wineglass that had already been poured for her and tossed its contents in Carter's face. "*Mad as hell* is more like it."

Carter's face turned red as he looked down at himself, his formerly pristine attire now splattered with wine. "What the hell did you do that for?"

"Getting even," she replied with some satisfaction, though she knew it was a far cry from what he'd done to her.

She turned on her heel and marched out, ignoring the stares of the other diners and the waitstaff.

She could practically hear the eggs in her ovaries aging with every step.

She'd been wrong, she realized. Work wasn't Carter's mistress. But something—or more accurately, *someone*—else was, she thought bitterly.

How could she not have seen Carter for what he was? Had her desperation for a child made her blind, shutting off her intuition?

As a professional party planner, she prided herself on being able to read people.

She made her way across the pavement to her car, a glower marring her features.

Betrayed by Carter, deceived by her father and dealt the crowning blow by Griffin. She should just wash her hands of the other half of the species and enter a nunnery, she thought with disgust.

And how dare Carter try to turn the tables on her by suggesting something was going on between her and Griffin?

Unbidden, her mind returned to Griffin's surprising kiss at her condo.

She'd been immobilized, stupefied by the passion lurking underneath Griffin's impassive facade.

For the first time, she sensed there was something, well, *untamed* about him. As if, underneath the power ties, custom suits and debonair tuxes, there was a man waiting to devour her.

And when he'd driven off yesterday, she'd noted he was now driving a Porsche—not what she would have expected from someone she'd thought of as buttoned-down.

Since yesterday, when her thoughts hadn't been filled with rage at Carter, she'd thought about *why* Griffin had kissed her.

She'd decided, because it was the only explanation that made any sense, that the kiss was just part of Griffin's high-handedness. He'd put an end to her taunts and baiting in the quickest way possible.

It *couldn't* be the case Griffin was attracted to her. They'd always rubbed each other the wrong way.

And even if, as was unlikely, Griffin was up for a roll between the sheets with her, it couldn't have anything to do with emotions. It would be either just sex, or laden with ulterior motives.

And the last thing she needed in her life right now was another man with ulterior motives.

"The wedding is off," she said flatly. "I wanted you to hear the news from me."

It was one of the most painful admissions of her life. But she knew she owed it to her parents to give them the news herself rather than have it catch up with them through the grapevine.

"Oh, Eva!" her mother said, before hurrying over for a hug.

Her father looked relieved, but he asked gruffly, "Are you okay?"

She'd driven directly to Mill Valley from the The Last Supper Club. When she'd arrived, she'd found her parents ensconced in their living room, where they'd obviously retired after dinner. Her mother, it had pained her to note, had been flipping through a bridal magazine. Her father had been watching a news show on television.

Now, Eva pulled away from her mother's embrace and faced her father. "You should be happy. Carter isn't going to be your son-in-law."

"*Happy* doesn't describe what I'm feeling at the moment."

"Elated?"

"What happened?"

"Griffin hasn't told you?" she said, feigning surprise. "Isn't the hired gun supposed to let his principal know the news first?"

Though Griffin had told her yesterday he'd come to her first with his evidence, she was surprised he hadn't immediately followed up with a call to Marcus. He'd left before she could ask him to let her break the news to her father herself, assuming her pride would have let her make such a request.

Her father had the grace to look a little uncomfortable. "He hasn't said a thing."

"Surprising since you *ordered* him to have Carter investigated," Eva responded coolly.

"In the first place, no one *orders* Griffin—"

"Marcus, is this true?" her mother interrupted, looking shocked.

Her father shifted his focus to her mother. "What else was I supposed to do, Audrey? He was about to marry into this family. And don't second-guess me, because Eva just admitted I was right!"

"Right about what?" her mother asked.

Eva sighed inwardly. "About Carter wanting to marry me for my money, Mom."

"Oh, Eva! I'm so sorry."

Her father muttered a few choice words.

She didn't want to bring up that, on top of it all, Carter had been cheating on her. Griffin's silence had given her an out, and she wasn't above using it now.

"What would you like us to tell everyone, Eva?" her mother asked quietly.

"Just tell them Carter and I decided to break up. *Period.*"

She'd thought about the issue on the drive over to her parents' place, and realized there were only a few people she wanted to share the whole truth with.

Fortunately, because her engagement to Carter hadn't yet become official—there'd been no ring, no party and no public announcement—there would be fewer questions. She also knew the last thing Carter would want to admit was that he'd been dumped by the heiress to the Tremont fortune because he'd been cheating on her.

Now she faced her father squarely. "I got rid of Carter, but you're my father and I can't change that."

Her father went still.

"So I'm just here to say," she continued, "*don't interfere in my life again.*"

"*Evangeline—*"

"And to use Griffin Slater, of all people."

Her father shook his head. "I never understood your aversion to Griffin."

"You know, I've never quite understood it myself. After all," she said sarcastically, "he's done me a favor by taking on the role for the Tremont heir that I'm not inclined to—or should I say, I'm not capable of?"

"I never said you were incapable."

"You didn't have to," she responded.

Her father looked stormy, while her mother simply seemed distressed.

"The reason I never pushed you toward Tremont REH," her father said, "is that I wanted you to be able to choose your own path and follow your own dreams."

The admission was a balm to raw feelings. Still, she wasn't letting him off the hook as far as Griffin was concerned.

"You may never have pushed me toward Tremont REH, but you're happy to push me at Griffin," she accused.

"Not because of Tremont REH," her father replied stubbornly, "but because he's a good man."

"Stop it, the both of you," her mother said, then turned her head toward her. "Eva, I hope you'll spend the night here. I hate to think of you being alone right now."

She was grateful for her mother's invitation, but she had one more thing to say to her father.

"Well, know this. Griffin Slater is the last man on earth I'd marry."

She thought it was a good parting shot. Especially since the risk of having to eat her words was zero.

Five

Two days after Griffin went to see Eva at her apartment, he looked up to see Marcus in the doorway of his office at work.

Usually Marcus's appearance at Tremont REH and Evkit's shared headquarters wasn't noteworthy. Only semiretired, he was in the habit of dropping in on a regular basis.

But this time Griffin knew better than to think Marcus's presence at work was unremarkable.

As Marcus shut the door behind him, his face turned into a glower. "That bastard, Newell."

His sentiments exactly, Griffin thought.

"Still, I'm glad Eva called off the wedding."

Griffin let the news of the cancelled nuptials wash over him like a cool wave on a blistering day. As mad as she'd been, at least Eva had had the good sense to give Carter the kiss-off.

He stood and came around his desk. "Glad you're focusing on the bottom line, Marcus."

"She said Ron found evidence Carter was marrying her for her money," the older man stated.

"Yes," Griffin said, not knowing how much Eva had revealed.

"How did he draw that conclusion?"

Griffin forced himself to shrug nonchalantly. "The usual stuff. A financial profile that showed Carter's living on a borrowed dime. Some interesting conversations caught on tape."

Since Marcus hadn't yet said anything about Carter two-timing Eva, Griffin kept his mouth shut on the topic.

Marcus nodded, looking, in fact, as if he didn't want Griffin to go into further detail.

Griffin didn't blame him. He wished *he* didn't know the particulars. He could only assume the situation was even more uncomfortable for Marcus, given that Eva was his daughter and only child.

"I went to Eva first," Griffin explained, skirting the issue of when exactly he'd gotten news from

Ron, "because I thought she was entitled to hear the information before anyone else. I figured she'd want to tell you herself."

"I appreciate your sticking your neck out here, Griffin." The older man gave him a wry smile. "Eva probably wants to have us both fried, so I'm glad she got the news first, at least. There's no sense jumping out of the frying pan and into the fire, eh?"

"Hang on to the thought."

"That's not the only thought I'm hanging on to," the older man continued. "She told her mother she threw wine in Newell's face when she confronted him."

Griffin took grim satisfaction in the knowledge Eva had rallied and shown the grit he knew her capable of instead of moping over Newell.

He worried about her, even though she sometimes made him nuts. His concern for her was ultimately what had made him comfortable with Marcus's request to have Newell investigated.

And that was also why he'd kissed her in her apartment—or so he'd told himself.

Let her think he was despicable, grabbing her for an inexplicable kiss at her vulnerable moment. At least it had kept her from spilling more unnecessary tears and engaging in misspent heartache.

When Marcus left his office moments later, Griffin's phone rang.

He picked up, and the voice at the other end said, "Just where I thought I'd find you—tied to your desk. Working too hard still?"

Griffin rubbed his neck. It was always good to hear from his brother.

"Just moving pieces around the Monopoly board," he quipped. "How are things going in the OR, kid?"

His brother laughed. "Seen one appendix, seen them all. But that's not why I'm calling."

"Oh, yeah?"

"Tessa is pregnant."

"Good Lord." He faked a groan. "You a father."

"From you, I'll take that as a compliment," his brother shot back.

Griffin found himself smiling. "Seriously, congratulations. Fantastic news."

"Thanks. We're thrilled."

"First Monica, now you. Well, at least you and Monica will have something in common for once in your lives."

Josh laughed. "You're making me shudder."

As he and his brother chatted about his sister-in-law's pregnancy, and the excitement about the upcoming arrival, Griffin's mind traveled back to Eva's declaration yesterday.

I'll never have a baby now.

He'd brooded over her words all last night.

He'd intended to save her from a two-timing fortune hunter. He hadn't realized he'd also be throwing a wrecking ball into her plans to beat her biological clock.

What the hell. Eva was only thirty-two. Plenty of women had children in their thirties, especially these days.

He'd looked up *premature menopause* on the Internet last night and had discovered it referred to women going into menopause in their thirties or even twenties. Some women were apparently genetically disposed to having their periods stop early, and from what Eva had said about her mother, Griffin concluded she was one of them.

"Hey, Griffin, you still there?" his brother asked, his voice exasperated but tinged with amusement.

Griffin realized he'd let his mind drift off.

"Yeah, sorry," he responded. "Listen, you and Tessa should come up to San Fran again soon. We'll celebrate. In fact, I've been thinking of throwing a little cocktail party for some business associates in a couple of weeks. It'd be great if I could coax you and Monica up here along with the spouses."

"I've got to check our schedule," Josh replied, "but I'm sure Tessa would love to travel as much as she can before the doctor grounds her for the last months of her pregnancy."

"Excellent."

"Putting that big house of yours to good use, huh?" his brother teased. "I've been wondering what you've been doing besides rattling around in it."

"Saving it for all the nephews and nieces that you and Monica are going to give me," he responded smoothly.

His brother snorted in disbelief. "Yeah, right. One day your wild harem parties are going to come to light."

His brother's teasing was a running joke between them. The truth was he'd lived life with a single-minded ambition since their parents had died.

When he signed off on his call with Josh, Griffin swiveled his chair to stare out his office windows.

He was happy for his brother, but it hammered home to him Eva's problem. *The problem he'd helped create for her.*

I'll never have a baby now.

For years, his attraction to Eva had been like a mild irritation—an itch he could avoid scratching if he put his mind to it.

And he *had* put his mind to it. He'd been focused on building his company and on parenting his younger siblings.

The last thing he'd needed was to get involved with his mentor's daughter and the ensuing *complications*.

But now that he'd scaled the mountain he'd set himself to climbing, he was able to stop and look around—and realize that maybe he'd fought his attraction to Eva for too long.

That he'd almost lost her to a worthless cad like Newell brought that last thought home to him.

Obviously Eva couldn't be trusted to make a sane decision about men, and by God, if she'd settle for Newell, she'd settle for him.

Griffin scanned the glittering crowd clustered on the terrace and lawn, and recognized most of the guests as regulars on San Francisco's society circuit. He supposed Eva knew many of them—some of them doubtlessly since her private school or Junior League days.

Weeks ago, he'd received an invitation to tonight's 1930s-themed party at the Palo Alto estate of socialite Beth Harding and her husband, Silicon Valley mogul Oliver Harding.

He'd initially decided not to attend, even though he and Oliver were acquainted from sitting on a couple of corporate boards together.

Right before the RSVP deadline, however, he'd changed his mind. He knew Beth was a good friend of Eva's, and Marcus had mentioned weeks ago that Eva was the party planner for tonight's event.

He hadn't seen Eva since last week, when he'd had to break the ugly news of Carter's infidelity to her, but he was determined to catch up with her.

So here he was, dressed in a zoot suit that he'd bought on the Internet, and feeling just a little ridiculous.

When he'd arrived a short time ago, the party had been well under way. Oliver had introduced him to Noah Whittaker, who was on a business trip to Silicon Valley for computer giant Whittaker Enterprises, and he'd spent some time talking business with the Boston-based entrepreneur.

He'd also gleaned from Oliver that Eva was mingling with the guests when she wasn't in the kitchen. She was apparently walking a line between hired help and invited guest.

He raised his glass of wine to his lips and scanned the crowd again—then paused as he finally spotted her.

His pulse kicked up.

She was wearing a black cigar girl's outfit. The tiny skirt reached to midthigh on her, revealing a set of shapely legs that went on forever. Fishnet stockings and platform peep-toe heels complemented the outfit.

She carried a small tray in front of her, suspended from a ribbon around her neck.

Clever, Griffin thought, even as desire heated his blood.

This was the first party he'd ever attended that had been organized by Eva. He wondered now whether he'd been too quick to judge and dismiss her business—and how good she was at it.

Absently he gave his wineglass to a passing waiter. Then he made his way toward her.

She was oblivious to his approach, but he reached her just as she began to move in the opposite direction.

"Making sure everything is going smoothly?" he asked before she could move out of earshot.

She whirled around.

Her eyes widened, and then narrowed. "In my work life you mean? Because as you know, my personal life is a mess at the moment."

He gave a curt nod, and she pretended to look him over.

"What? No more shocking photos?" she baited him. "No more sensational evidence?"

"I heard you gave Carter the boot."

"From my father, no doubt."

"You didn't completely explain to him why, though."

She tilted her head. "Disappointed that I've been spared the ultimate humiliation?"

"I wouldn't say that. I can think of worse things—"

"—than telling my father he was more than right?" she finished for him mockingly. "That Carter was cheating on me?"

"Your father does care about you, Eva."

He glimpsed sudden and unexpected emotion in her eyes.

"Yes, I know, but sometimes that doesn't help," she responded finally. "Now, if you'll excuse me, I've got a job to do."

He reached out and captured her elbow. "The party's winding down."

She glanced down at his hand on her elbow, then back up at him. "Take your hand off me."

He ignored her. "We both know you're as much a guest here as anything, and at this point in the evening, your job is basically done. You can spare a few minutes."

She looked exasperated. "You don't quit, do you?"

His lips quirked. "Someday, you may come to appreciate that as one of my finer qualities."

"I doubt it. Though considering how few fine qualities you possess, on second thought, maybe the idea isn't so far-fetched."

"Are you going to stand there throwing verbal poisoned darts at me, or can we step aside and talk for a few minutes?"

She lifted her brows. "I'm surprised it's taken you this long to catch up with me."

"You're a difficult woman to get hold of."

He'd purposely shown up late to the party, because he was here for one purpose only.

"Fine," she responded. "Follow me."

Following her entailed winding their way past assorted guests. Some of them attempted to get Eva's attention or his, but Eva was determined not to be detained for more than a few moments, and he, likewise, was set on not having their progress halted.

Eva stopped when they made it inside to the kitchen. She removed the tray from around her neck as various employees hustled past them, bearing food in and out of the kitchen.

Griffin counted gangsters, chorus girls, office girls and, yes, cigar girls.

Eva folded her arms. "Shoot."

He glanced around. "I was thinking of some place more private."

"Too bad. This is all I have time for."

On closer inspection, he noticed her face looked strained. As if she hadn't been sleeping well.

He silently cursed Carter Newell—and for good

measure, damned his own role in bringing Newell's transgressions to Eva's attention.

His lips tightened. "I created this problem."

Eva frowned. "What problem?"

"Your broken engagement."

She spread her hands. "Look, Griffin, I know what I said last week, but I'm an adult. Now that the initial shock has passed, I know enough not to blame the messenger—"

"I'm not talking about Carter," he interrupted.

"Well, good—but what are you talking about then?"

"I'm talking about throwing a wrench in your plans to beat the biological clock."

She tilted her head. "Yes, well…that was an unintended consequence, wasn't it?"

"What are you going to do?" he asked bluntly. The issue had been bothering him since last week. *A lot.*

She sighed, looking weary and vulnerable. "I don't know yet."

"Have dinner with me tomorrow night," he offered without preamble.

Her eyes widened a fraction, pools of golden-amber. "I can't."

"Why not? Do you have to work?"

"No…tonight is the only time I have to work this weekend."

"Then have dinner with me."

"Why?" she asked, suspicion darkening her tone. "So you can ambush me with more disturbing news?"

"Unfair. You know better."

"Then why?"

He shrugged and shoved his hands in his pockets. "Maybe I'm interested in stepping up to the plate."

Her eyes widened for real this time. "What?"

"You want a baby, and I'm the guy who created your present problem," he said evenly.

A half laugh escaped her, her expression disbelieving.

"Don't you think your boss would frown on your knocking up his daughter?" she asked tartly.

He felt a smile tug at his lips. "In the first place, your father is really no longer my employer. In the second, I'm offering to do this right. Marriage."

She looked stunned, but she recovered quickly. "Isn't it a bit much to be volunteering to fix things this way?"

"Why don't you let me worry about that part?"

Her lips parted. "There's no spark between us."

"I disagree."

The words hung in the air between them, and he could tell she was remembering the kiss they'd shared at her apartment, just as he hadn't been able to forget it, either.

She laughed again, but it came out a trifle forced. Then she moved to step by him. "Griffin, be serious."

"I am," he said, blocking her with his arm when she was very close.

She looked up at him mutely.

"Why don't we kiss and put it to the test?"

A flash of alarm crossed her face.

"I don't think—"

"That's right, *don't think,*" he parried.

And before she could say anything more, he swept her into his arms.

Six

Any hope she'd had that she could chalk up last week's embrace as an aberration was vaporized by the heat of their kiss.

It sizzled along her nerve endings, danced along the surface of her skin and pooled as throbbing need between her legs.

Griffin cupped the back of her head, slanted his mouth and deepened the kiss, giving her his tongue.

Rock-hard planes pressed against her, and his mouth tasted of wine and man.

It was like being consumed, Eva thought dimly. Unwrapped, exposed and thoroughly enjoyed.

She moaned low in her throat…and a moment later heard a whistle of encouragement.

Abruptly she was brought back to earth.

She pushed Griffin away, and her gaze landed on the amused expressions of two of the waitstaff.

Clearly she and Griffin had been providing some free entertainment.

She compressed her lips. She should be setting an example for her employees, not engaging in teenage antics.

She touched Griffin's arm and said tightly, "Come with me."

She knew there was a study across the hall from the kitchen, and it was likely empty since the party was taking place mostly outside.

She led the way, and once inside, she shut the door behind them.

Table lamps cast a warm yellow glow, lighting a room done in dark hues, from the maroon leather chair to the gray sofa facing the fireplace.

She faced Griffin. "So is today's performance your coda to a carefully constructed plan to ruin my life?"

He raised his eyebrows, his expression mild.

She started counting off on her fingers. "Let's see. Last week, you informed me that my fiancé was cheating on me. This week, you grab me for an adolescent tussle in front of my employees."

He had the indecency to let his lips to twitch.

"I needed to grab your attention," he said. "I succeeded."

She ignored the flutter in her stomach. "I have options, you know."

So what if she sounded defensive? This whole conversation was ridiculous. She couldn't believe she was even discussing the topic of conceiving a child with Griffin Slater.

Except his proposition was so ludicrous, she was having a hard time coming up with a sane way to refute it. So instead of addressing the sticky issues—such as their complete incompatibility— she went for the straightforward one.

She regarded him coolly. "It's possible to just buy a vial of sperm over the Internet these days. Why do I need you when I'm capable of getting pregnant on my own?"

He eyed her. "Do you really want to be a single parent?"

What she really wanted was to be loved for herself, she thought, but squelched the wayward thought. "I could have my eggs frozen until I met someone."

"Egg freezing technology is still experimental. Besides, you could be waiting years to be a parent."

She was surprised he knew about egg freezing, but she supposed he'd read a news report somewhere.

"I'd be a father to your child. To *our* child," he continued. "Today. Tomorrow."

Damn him. He was holding out everything she wanted on a silver platter. Well, almost everything.

Her silly heart ached, and she automatically sought to protect it. It had been getting a pounding recently.

"What's in this for you?" she asked suspiciously.

"With any luck, I'll get a child—a child who will one day inherit Tremont REH."

She frowned. "How are you any different from Carter then? He had ulterior motives that involved getting his hands on Tremont REH money and so do you."

He looked as if she'd insulted him. "In the first place, I'm being up-front with you. Our marriage would have advantages for both of us. Secondly, I don't want Tremont REH for myself." He shrugged. "But I'd be happy if a child of ours inherited that legacy."

She was surprised he didn't claim he was entitled to get his hands on Tremont REH by virtue of his having contributed to its success, and grudgingly conceded it was a point in his favor.

At the same time, she knew she had to get away *now,* because her abused heart just couldn't take any more.

She'd spent her whole life trying to create an

identity for herself apart from being *the Tremont heiress*—real estate mogul Marcus Tremont's daughter. It had been a futile effort, but she hated the way it always caught up with her—particularly now.

She reached for the doorknob. "I need to get back."

Griffin stepped forward, his gaze intent. "Eva—"

Just then, however, the door was pushed open, and she took a step back, her hand falling away from the knob.

One of her employees, dressed as a 1930s-era doctor, complete with head mirror and suspenders, appeared in the doorway.

"Here you are!" he said. "We've all been looking for you! Sue wants to know where Beth Harding's spare freezer is located."

She chanced one more look at Griffin. "I've got to go."

Then she ducked out of the room.

She wasn't fleeing…or so she tried to convince herself.

"He what?" Beth Harding asked.

"He proposed to me," Eva repeated. Saying the words made them only slightly more real.

She leaned back against the cushions of her couch and set her coffee cup down on the end table. She was still in her pajamas, having allowed herself the luxury of sleeping in after having worked at the Hardings' party.

Beth laughed. "Well that was quick work. Last week, he got rid of your fiancé and this week he proposes to you himself!"

"In a sense."

She'd filled in Beth about Carter's deceit and Griffin's role in bringing it to her attention. She'd left out the kiss with Griffin at her apartment because, she told herself, she'd chalked it up as an aberration.

But there was no way to chalk up *a proposal* as an anomaly or a figment of her imagination—though she'd tried last night. If she'd been successful, she'd have been able to dismiss the strange temptations she was feeling.

And when Beth had phoned this morning to discuss how the party had gone, she couldn't help but tell her friend about the *real* entertainment last night.

"I'll say this for him," Beth said. "He's slow out of the gate, but he sure knows how to make up for lost time. He's known you, what? Ten years?"

"Has it been that long?" she responded.

"So what are you going to do?" Beth asked.

"Are you kidding? Nothing! In case it's escaped your notice, I've spent the last decade detesting Griffin Slater."

"There's a fine line between love and hate."

Didn't she know it. The past few days had brought that home to her. She'd thought she loved Carter, only to discover she hadn't known him at all. And she'd thought she detested Griffin, only to discover, well...

But she didn't want to go there with Beth. "Anyway, I don't need him. This is the twenty-first century. I have options. Except, of course, he very considerately pointed out to me that, by taking him up on his *proposal,* I wouldn't get just a sperm donor, but an involved father."

"He's got a point there."

"Thanks a lot."

"I'm just saying. I've got three kids, and believe me, there are days when I'd like to clone myself."

"Hmm."

A buzz sounded, indicating there was an incoming call on her cell phone. She removed the phone from her ear to check the screen, and recognized the number as Griffin's. Over the years, they'd been in perfunctory phone contact about Tremont REH board business, so she wasn't surprised he had her number.

Speaking into the phone again, she said to Beth, "You won't believe this, but it's Griffin on the other line. Can I talk to you later?"

"Of course! Let me know how it goes. I'll be dying to know if he drops any other shocks on you. Oliver is so boring!"

When she'd ended the call with Beth, and switched over to the other call, she said unnecessarily, "Hello?"

"It's Griffin."

"I suppose you're calling to recant your moment of insanity last night," she said, affecting a bored tone, even though she was experiencing the exhilaration of a sky dive. "Well, no need to bother—"

"Actually," he interrupted dryly, "I'm calling to hire you for a party."

She sighed. "I feel compelled to point out that, as your spouse, you'd get my services for free. So, I'm confused—have you decided to hedge your bets?"

He laughed. "Okay, you're on to me. My diabolic plan is to force you, one way or another, to provide me with a free party whenever I want."

"I've got news for you," she shot back. "It would hardly be a party."

He chuckled. "I think I could handle you."

A wave of heat sizzled through her.

"I really am calling to hire you," he insisted. "I've been thinking of throwing a cocktail party for some business associates a week from Friday."

"Oh."

"Are you available?"

"I need to check my calendar." She already knew she was free.

"I was planning to go with the caterer I usually use, nothing fancy, but after seeing you in action last night, I wanted to hire Occasions by Designs."

"I don't come cheap."

"Do you really want my answer to that?"

"You are persistent."

"My middle name. And how can you resist the opportunity to prove to me how good you are?" he said, his voice low and smooth as silk.

Damn him, he knew how to get to her.

Aloud, she said crisply, "We'll have to discuss what you want, and I'll have to send you my standard contract."

"Excellent."

When she ended her call with Griffin, she immediately thought that she was going to regret agreeing to this assignment.

Before she could dwell on her anxiety, however, her phone rang again, playing "That's What Friends Are For."

She flicked the cell open. "Hello, Beth."

"Well?" her friend asked. "How did it go? I decided calling was better than dying to find out."

"He wants to hire me."

"Rent-a-wife?"

"No, another stunner. He wants me to arrange a party for him. I can't tell anymore if he's lusting after me or Occasions by Design."

"Well, I give him points for originality. It's better than lusting for the Tremont REH millions."

Actually, Griffin was keeping her so off balance, Eva thought, that she wasn't sure what he was really after.

As she filled in Beth about her phone call with Griffin, she also realized that, for once in her life, she could see a positive side to being pursued for her money by men like Carter: at least she knew where she stood.

Eva arrived at Griffin's Pacific Heights mansion at four on a bright Friday afternoon. She had given herself three hours to set up before the guests arrived.

From the curb, Eva looked up at the house's impressive Queen Anne facade, which was partially shielded from the street by a high fence and well-manicured front garden.

When Griffin had given her his address over the phone last week, so she could set up deliveries for the party, she hadn't thought twice about his location in Pacific Heights.

Now, however, she was surprised to discover he

lived in a majestic structure replete with gables, wings and towers.

She was charmed despite herself.

Over the years, she'd made a point not to be curious about Griffin. The less she knew about him, the more she could pretend not to be affected by him. And because they'd ironed out the details of tonight's party by phone and fax, she'd never had the opportunity to see his home until today.

She'd been relieved, actually, by the indirect communication. These days, she didn't think she could take another face-to-face encounter with Griffin.

But she knew her reprieve was about to come to an end.

As some of her employees unloaded supplies from one of Occasions by Design's vans, Griffin drove up in his silver sports car.

She watched him park at the curb. Seconds later, he emerged, pushing back black sunglasses to the top of his head.

She took in his navy-blue suit, and noted he looked as if he'd gotten a haircut. His hair, short to begin with, now thinly outlined his uncompromisingly masculine face.

He looked crisp, sexy…spectacular.

Her body vibrated with energy. It was a reaction she was growing used to now that she knew the reaction he was able to evoke from her with his lips and his hands.

Still, she was determined to resist him. Tonight was about scoring another hit for Occasions by Design. Nothing else.

She told herself she was here simply because she had room in her calendar to arrange this party. Of course, after the Carter debacle—how could she have been so blind?—it was also possible she was a master of self-deception.

Luckily her parents weren't going to be here tonight, so the pressure was off in that regard. She knew from her mother that her parents had had to decline Griffin's invitation because they'd a prior commitment.

"Hello," Griffin called, his gaze sweeping over her.

She felt his look like a hot stamp, and she smoothed her hand over a crease in her trousers. She was dressed in an outfit she loved—a beaded, corn-flower-blue top, black silk pants and Christian Louboutin mules—but she suddenly felt self-conscious.

To cover her nervousness, she nodded to the mansion before them. "Not quite where I pictured you living."

A slow smile spread across his face as he came closer. "Let me guess. You were expecting some penthouse condo bachelor pad."

She nodded. "I thought I heard my father mention a while back that you had a place somewhere downtown."

"I gave up the penthouse a couple of years ago." He shrugged. "I was looking for a change. And this place allows me to entertain on a larger scale. It's still a work in progress, though."

"Two years ago?" she asked. "Wasn't that around the time you got your promotion to CEO of Tremont REH?"

She was being contrary by implying Tremont money was the reason he could afford a fancy Pacific Heights address, but she couldn't help herself.

Anything to divert the heat of his gaze from her. She felt as if she could go up in flames right here on the pavement.

"Let's just say, the real estate market was doing well at the time," he returned easily. "For Evkit Investments as well as Tremont REH."

"I just assumed a penthouse would be more your speed," she said in a more conciliatory tone. "You must be lost in all this space."

An enigmatic smile played at his lips. "Hoping for evidence in my choice of real estate that I'm not the settling down type? Sorry to disappoint."

"Actually," she parried, "I thought you'd enjoy the

view from up high in a penthouse, looking down at us lesser mortals."

He chuckled, and then murmured, "I don't think you have a clue what I'd *enjoy,* Evangeline."

Eva realized they were no longer talking about real estate—or even the seriousness of his marriage proposal.

A vision of the two of them having sex on tangled sheets sprang into her mind.

Reflexively she shook her head to clear it.

"Is something wrong?" he asked, his expression amused and too knowing.

She whirled away. "I need to go supervise in the kitchen since there's not much time. I'm here to plan a party, remember?"

"Of course," he murmured as she turned away. "Why else would you be here?"

His cryptic comment almost broke her stride, but she forced herself to keep going.

His question echoed in her head. *Why else would she be here?*

Seven

So far so good, Eva thought, as she made sure plates and utensils continued to be well stocked on a sideboard set up in Griffin's living room.

It dawned on her that she didn't feel like a professional party planner tonight, or even a guest.

Instead it felt as if she and Griffin were joint hosts, acting in easy, unspoken harmony. She'd helped welcome his guests, many of whom she happened to be acquainted with, and Griffin had come back to the kitchen to assist several times. It was almost as if they were *husband and wife,* a voice in her head whispered before she could silence it.

Earlier in the evening, she'd been just as charmed by the inside of Griffin's house as by the outside. The chef's kitchen—with its top-of-the-line stainless steel appliances, granite countertops, double sink and two cooking ranges—was a dream. The layout of the other rooms on the ground floor lent itself to the easy flow of traffic. French doors and a large number of windows also brought in a nice breeze to the party.

There was no doubt about it, she reflected as she straightened up the sideboard. Griffin had chosen well when he'd purchased the house. But then she supposed she shouldn't be surprised he had a keen eye for real estate.

She'd also had to concede tonight that Griffin was far wealthier than she'd imagined.

It wasn't just the impressiveness of his home. From snatches of conversation among the guests, she'd discovered just how successful Evkit Investments had become in the last few years—years during which she'd purposely refused to pay attention to anything Griffin was doing.

Many guests had heaped praise on Griffin's investment savvy. She'd learned that Griffin owned prime residential real estate—condos and rental units, alike—all over San Francisco.

Union Square. Russian Hill. Bernal Heights.

Fisherman's Wharf. And, of course, Pacific Heights. His acquisitions ran the gamut of San Francisco's exclusive and hot neighborhoods.

Under other circumstances, the guests' conversation may have driven her crazy. Tonight, however, it didn't bother her. She was more consumed with Griffin's effect on her pulse whenever he was nearby.

She stole a look at him now across the room, where he stood by the mantel chatting with a middle-aged couple and holding a wineglass by the stem.

He'd changed into an open-collar white shirt and black pants for the party, but even in casual attire, his seductive allure made her heart trip over itself.

"Eva."

Startled from her reverie, she turned and noticed Griffin's sister coming toward her.

"Monica! I haven't seen you in ages."

Monica gave her a relieved smile. "I'm just glad I'm here. Ben had to be in San Fran for a business dinner tonight, but we thought we'd stop by Griffin's afterward for the end of the party."

Eva knew Griffin's sister had gotten married a couple of years ago to a Hollywood film producer and now spent most of her time in L.A.

She hugged Monica, and felt an unmistakable bump below the other woman's baby doll top. Pulling back, she said, "You're—?"

Monica nodded, her face glowing. "We're thrilled."

"Griffin didn't say a thing," she exclaimed. Though she was happy for Monica, her heart did a sad little clench over the fact that her own dream of a family had lately become more elusive.

Monica smiled again. "I told Griffin a while back, but you know, sometimes he can be so... What's the word I'm looking for?"

"Arrogant? Irritating? Unbearable?"

Monica laughed. "You know him so well!"

And even better lately, Eva thought.

Monica looked over at her brother. "I just hope he's okay. He spent so many years watching over me and Josh that I wonder whether he's feeling a little adrift these days."

She knew the story of Griffin's parents' untimely death, of course, but for as long as she'd known him, Griffin had always seemed strong and invincible.

"I can think of many words for your brother, but *adrift* isn't one of them," she said. Where she was concerned, at least, Griffin was all too confident about what he wanted.

She glanced over at Griffin, and when his eyes met hers across the room, she sucked in a breath.

Deliberately she turned back toward his sister.

"I'm serious," Monica continued. "Sometimes, I wonder whether restlessness is the reason Griffin bought this house. He was paying tuition bills and dealing with orthodontist appointments at a time when many college guys are only thinking about the next keg party. Now he doesn't know what to do with himself."

Monica's words made Eva think about Griffin's offer to get married. Was he just restless? Or was he feeling left out now that his siblings were wed?

Monica touched her arm. "Let's talk about lighter subjects. How are you? And how is—oh, wait, what is his name?—*Carter?*"

"Gone," she replied succinctly.

From Monica's question, Eva surmised that Griffin hadn't filled in his sister about any of the sorry details of her life lately. The last time she'd seen Monica, months ago, she'd just begun dating Carter.

A line marred Monica's brow. "Oh, I'm sorry."

"Don't be," she replied. "It ended badly, but it's all for the best."

A wry smile touched Monica's lips. "I'm not good at picking lighter subjects, am I?"

Eva felt an answering smile pull at her mouth. "Don't worry about it."

"Have you had a chance to see the house?" Monica asked, changing the subject. "Its details are glorious. You should have Griffin show you around when the party is over."

"It would be nice, but I'm sure he'll be tired by the end of the evening," she responded, thinking Monica had no reason to believe Griffin's house *wasn't* a safe topic of conversation for her.

She was spared saying more, however, because Monica's husband, Ben, joined them and the conversation abruptly veered in a different direction.

A short time later, she was called away to supervise cleanup in the kitchen as the guests began to depart. She arranged for the leftover food to go to a homeless shelter, as she usually did.

And she let her last employees leave just as she began to double-check the kitchen to make sure it had been restored to normal.

Griffin entered the kitchen as she was placing a couple of utensils in a drawer.

"Monica and Josh and company just left," he announced.

She looked up and stopped what she was doing. They were alone in this big house together? Tension throbbed through her.

"I thought they'd be staying here," she blurted. "There's so much room."

"They've both kept the condos in San Fran that I bought for them several years ago." Griffin winked. "Much better than being under big brother's watchful eye."

"*Oh.* Well, I'm sorry I didn't have a chance to say goodbye," she responded.

Griffin had bought condos for his siblings? It was just another hint she'd gotten tonight of how well he'd taken care of Monica and Josh after their parents died.

"Monica knew you were busy in the kitchen and didn't want to bother you," Griffin said as he sauntered over to a kitchen counter and leaned against it. He looked relaxed, while she felt pinpricks of awareness on every inch of her skin.

As she wiped nonexistent crumbs off his kitchen counter, she said, "I understand congratulations are in order. You're going to be an uncle."

"Twice over," he replied. "Josh told me just a couple of weeks that ago he and Tessa are expecting, too."

The words hung in the air, calling forth the issues that stood between them—her quest for a child, and his offer, which she hadn't yet given a clear *yes* or *no* to.

She tossed a paper towel into the garbage can, and he said easily, "You know Monica commanded me to give you a tour of the house before you left."

"Did she?" she replied quickly. "It's really not necessary."

"I insist. The party was a great success thanks to you. You should at least get a tour of the house."

She didn't want to be drawn any more into the house's seductive allure—*his* seductive allure. She didn't want to picture herself here, and imagine redoing one of the rooms as a nursery.

He pushed away from the counter and grasped her hand.

The contact sent a little electric shock dancing up her arm.

This was Griffin, her disbelieving brain broadcast to her heart.

She'd known him forever. She'd disliked him for nearly as long.

"Come on," he said.

Eva let Griffin lead her through the kitchen and toward the front of the house.

She was already familiar in passing with most of the downstairs rooms, but Griffin identified them with a nod as they walked past through a central hall.

A formal dining room was followed by an oversize living room with a carved wood mantel. There was also a study lined with built-in bookshelves, a laundry and a room devoted solely to a large pool table. The pool room had made her pause when she'd spotted it earlier in the evening—Griffin, it seemed, was as devoted a pool player as her father.

The decor was a mix of Victorian traditional and comfortable contemporary that made up a thoroughly and distinctively West Coast aesthetic.

When they reached the front entry, Griffin turned and headed up the house's central staircase.

"You must have some help to maintain this place," she commented as they climbed.

"Yeah, but not live-in," he answered. "I use a housekeeping service here and for the cottage I've got in Napa."

Upstairs, he opened and closed doors, showing her the various bedrooms. One room still had the feminine rose-print wallpaper left by the previous owners. Another had two twin beds separated by a traditional Victorian vanity table. Two other rooms had yet to be furnished.

There were five bedrooms in all, and the master suite was last.

The final room took her by surprise with its casual ambiance. Griffin leaned against the doorjamb and watched as she looked around.

From the belongings scattered about, the bedroom looked *lived in,* unlike some of the other rooms of the house.

There was a large bed with a stunning black-lacquer frame and contrasting white linens. Sumptuous yellow silk curtains highlighted three large windows, and a patterned area rug covered the dark-stained wood floor.

"You approve?" he asked.

She nodded, knowing she had to get out of here before her pulse jumped through her skin. "The decor is lovely. The whole house is."

She moved toward the doorway, but he was filling it.

"I'm glad," he said, his voice low and rich.

"I need…"

To go.

But she never finished the thought, the words dying on her lips as he gazed at her intently.

He leaned toward her, searched her face and then lowered his mouth to hers.

This time she was expecting the tingle, the dizzying burst of euphoria.

He kissed her, hot and deep, pulling her into his arms. Her arms crept around his neck as their mouths tangled and the heat built.

The world faded away, and a flame of desire sparked within her.

"Mmm."

She belatedly realized the sound had come from her.

When he pulled away, his breathing was deep and her eyelids felt heavy.

"What are you doing?" she asked huskily.

"Isn't it obvious?"

"I'm here to do a job—"

"—that just ended. You don't work for me anymore."

She tried again. "I'm a party planner."

"Yeah…and do you want me to spell out how you can *really* throw a party for me?"

A sizzle went through her.

"Incredible, isn't it?" he asked, his voice rough with arousal. "We've known each other, what? A decade? If I'd known kissing you would be this good, I'd never have been able to resist."

Her parched heart soaked up his words greedily. It was desperate for a shower of sincerity after Carter's infidelity.

"There was no *resisting* involved," she contradicted huskily. "You didn't like me."

"If only that had been true."

Before she could say anything else, he kissed her again, and the passion flared immediately.

After a moment, she tore her mouth from his. "Wait. We can't do this!"

"Why?" he asked. "You shed a fiancé, and—" he glanced around them as if looking for someone "—ah, yes, I never had one."

"This is such a classic rebound scenario!"

His eyes bore into hers, obsidian disks promising pleasure. "It's hard to give a damn about that right now, but yeah, *okay*. Do you even care?"

"I—"

Lord, *she didn't*. It was hard to care, to think even, at the moment.

Why not sleep with Griffin? There didn't have to be any strings attached. He could be her fling after Carter. A salve to her ego.

Griffin nibbled at her lips. "Carter was an idiot. He couldn't see past your bank account to the woman you are."

His hand found the zipper of her beaded top and tugged. "Just take the plunge," he said, his voice low and coaxing. "What have you got to lose?"

"You're not the wild and crazy type," she pointed out.

"I'm a real estate investor. That makes me a gambler by nature."

Funny, she'd never thought of him that way. He'd always appeared too staid and buttoned-down to be the adventurous type. But lately she'd seen an entirely different side of Griffin.

Her top came apart in back, the two halves of the zipper parting. With a little assistance from Griffin, the top slid off her shoulders and down her arms to pool at her feet. She was left clad on top in only her demi-bra.

Griffin's eyes flared. "You're lovely, Eva."

He put his hands on her waist and then stroked up and down her rib cage, the pads of his thumbs skimming over the sensitized skin of her stomach.

She was acutely aware of his every movement. Still, she fought for a sophisticated insouciance she didn't feel.

"No strings, Griffin," she said flippantly. "Tonight you're my consolation fling, and that's all."

Griffin's jaw hardened. "If that's what you want."

"It's what I want," she confirmed, her fingers going to the buttons of his shirt and undoing the first one.

"Then why waste any more time?"

And with those words, he picked her up and strode to the bed.

He sat her down on his lap, and kissed her thoroughly.

She cupped the back of his head and returned his kiss without reservation. If she was going to throw caution to the wind, then she was going to make sure to enjoy herself thoroughly.

His erection pushed against her, fueling the aching need beginning to build inside her. His fingers delved into her hair, and she felt the strong beat of his heart against her.

Her black mules hit the floor, one after the other, and a moment later, she found herself sliding to her feet between his legs, helped along by his pat on her rear end.

Griffin nuzzled her breasts, and she drew him toward her, resting her arms on his shoulders as her hands cupped the back of his head.

With a flick of his wrist, he undid her bra and tossed it across the room.

He drew one nipple into his mouth, and lapped the peak with his tongue again and again, intermittently sucking gently.

Her knees went weak. "Oh, Griffin."

"Yes," he said thickly. "Enjoy."

He transferred his attention to her other breast, and she grew breathless, suffocated by passion.

When he finally lifted his head, she would have given him anything, but his fingers went to the waistband of her pants and he fumbled with the button and zipper.

Moments later, he pushed the pants down her hips, hooking his thumbs into the waistband of her panties along the way and taking those down as well.

He focused on the apex of her thighs and caressed it with the palm of his hand.

She went delirious with want. Tonight was so

wrong in every way that the taste of the forbidden fueled her desire.

His hands went to her waist, and, in a surprise move, he lifted her and tumbled her back onto the bed beside them.

He stood then, and holding her gaze, popped the buttons on his shirt and tossed the garment aside.

She felt the breath leave her.

Beneath his Clark Kent persona, Griffin was every woman's fantasy. His chest was washboard flat, and it was clear that before or after his time at the office, he worked out.

His eyelids hooded, Griffin watched her as he slid off his belt and kicked off his shoes.

She licked her lips. "The doctor said the tests came back clear."

"I'm glad," he said deeply. "I just let them run the blood work during my annual physical. I got a clean bill last month, in fact."

He lowered his pants and briefs, his erection springing free.

She couldn't remember ever being so excited in her life. "I— Uh, I'm still on the pill. I never went off, even though Carter and I decided to abstain for a while before the wedding."

She lifted a shoulder. "I guess I wanted to be sure we were safe until we were ready to try…"

She let the sentence trail off, but she was sure he understood what she meant. Until they were ready *to try to have a child.*

Griffin nodded, and then he picked up her leg and placed a kiss on the sensitive skin of her inner arch. "*Try* to relax. *Try* to enjoy this." A slow, wicked smile touched his lips. "*Try* to let me know how I'm making you feel."

He grasped her other ankle, pulled her to the edge of the bed and then began to pleasure her with his mouth.

It all happened so fast, she barely had time to utter a startled exclamation of surprise.

She turned her head to the side and brought her fist to her mouth to stifle her moan.

Carter had *never* shown any interest in pleasuring her this way. She was stunned by the thrilling new sensations coursing through her.

Griffin grasped her arm and pulled her hand from her mouth, raising his head long enough to say in a smoky voice, "Remember, *try* to let me know how you feel."

She *couldn't* let him know. Instead she kept trying to remember her motive for ending up in Griffin's bed.

Revenge affair, revenge affair, revenge affair.

That's all it was. A one-night stand to soothe her pride.

Just like that, however, shock waves racked her, and she felt herself splinter and come apart.

Griffin raised himself up and held her until her body relaxed again.

When he smoothed a stray hair away from her face, her eyes met his.

Her lips parted. "Carter never wanted to—"

"Carter is an idiot. Haven't we established that already?"

Despite his dark tone, his expression held masculine satisfaction—as if he was pleased he'd already outplayed Carter.

She slid her hand along his muscled thigh, giving in to the overwhelming urge to touch and caress him.

He tensed and caught her hand. "Ah, kitten. Not a good idea right now."

She looked at him questioningly, and then heated as understanding dawned.

"I've got to be inside you," he said roughly. "I'm right at the edge."

"Yes," she breathed.

He positioned her, and then slid inside her, inch by inch, filling up all the empty space within her.

When he entered her completely, he expelled an explosive breath.

She'd underestimated, Eva thought dimly, what it would be like to be possessed by Griffin.

He began to move in a steady rhythm, his hands and mouth working to evoke a response from her and having an unerring sense of where her pleasure points were.

Another orgasm racked her, her fingers digging into his back, but Griffin just kept taking her higher…until they hung there in the balance, a stretched moment of tension that let them savor the intimacy.

And then with a harsh groan, Griffin arched back, the tendons standing in relief against his neck, and drove into her, spilling himself inside of her and triggering her own final, blissful topple over the edge.

Eight

Griffin awoke the next morning with a smile on his lips. He had the pleasant sensation of emerging from the mists of an erotic dream.

As the last remnants of fog dissipated, last night came back to him.

He'd bedded Evangeline Tremont.

He'd never felt so connected during sex.

The bed shifted beside him, and he leaned over, propping himself on an elbow.

Eva's eyes remained closed but it was clear she was waking up.

Her midnight hair fanned out on the pillow, her

lashes inky against the milky softness of her skin. Her lips were parted and looked puffy, soft and inviting.

His mind replayed scenes from the night before. He remembered how passionately she'd kissed him back and how expertly she'd used her mouth—and he felt the stirrings of arousal.

Eva moved, and her leg slid against his.

After a moment, her eyes fluttered open.

"Good morning," he said.

"Er— Hi."

"I was just watching you wake up."

Her eyes widened. "Were you?"

"Last night was—" he searched for a word to do it justice, but settled on "—fantastic." He slid his hand down her leg in a leisurely caress. He'd enjoy a repeat of last night's performance right about now. In fact, he thought, focusing on her mouth, he couldn't think of a better way to spend the morning.

He leaned down to kiss her, but just as he was about to lower his mouth to hers, she tossed back the sheet and sprang out of bed.

He watched her, bemused. "Where are you going?"

At the same time, he couldn't help enjoying the view. She had a fantastic body. He pictured the photo he'd seen numerous times in Marcus's study: a teenage Eva, dressed in her ballet outfit and doing a pirouette.

Eva grabbed her bra and panties from the floor, and then glanced at the alarm clock on his bedside table. "It's Saturday. I—I've got to get to work. There's a function at the MOMA tonight."

"I'll be there."

"You're not invited."

"I've got connections," he teased. "And the most important is a certain well-known party planner."

She didn't answer. Instead she yanked on her panties, not sparing him a glance.

The easy amusement playing at the edges of his mouth died away. He was getting the distinct impression he was on the receiving end of a brush-off, and he didn't like it.

You're my consolation fling. Her words came back to him, though the night before they'd been lost in a haze of desire.

Like hell, he thought.

After what they'd shared, he wasn't about to let her dismiss them as a casual *anything.*

He threw back the covers on his side of the bed, and stood up.

She put on her bra as he prowled toward her.

"Leaving so soon?" he asked.

She looked around the floor. "I—I've got to find my shoes."

When she bent to search, he grasped her forearm and stopped her. "I'm not going to let you run from this."

She tossed her hair back as she straightened. "I don't know what you mean."

"I mean, you're scared and you're running, Evangeline."

"Scared of what? *You?*" she asked scornfully. "I'm not Little Red Riding Hood and you're not the Big Bad Wolf."

"That's too bad," he responded, "because I'm definitely hungry for you."

Last night, he'd just about devoured her.

She paled, but recovered her bravado quickly. "Let's not make last night into more than it was, okay? Thanks for helping to restore my confidence after Carter. You can check it off your list."

"Great," he said smoothly. "Now let's run off to Vegas and elope. I'll check that item off my list, and your revenge will be complete."

"What?"

She stared at him in such open astonishment, he almost laughed.

"You're crazy!"

He arched a brow. "I'm offering you a way to walk away from Carter and get the last word. A way to get everything you want, including a baby. But you're turning me down. So who's crazy?"

"Both your siblings are having kids," she tossed back, her tone tinged with suspicion. "Is that the reason you're so willing to have a child with me? Because you're feeling left out?"

His jaw set. "Let's just say I had a chance recently to discover what I really wanted."

He'd gotten a wake-up call, all right. Just not in the way she believed. The fact that she'd almost slipped through his hands and fallen into Newell's had been his reveille.

Now, he saw emotion flicker in her eyes, and sensed a weakening of her defenses.

He pressed forward. "What have you got to lose?"

They both knew her fiancé was gone, and her prospects for going out and getting another one anytime soon were dim.

"I can't elope!" she exclaimed abruptly. "I'm a party planner!"

He gave a bark of laughter, and then pulled her into his arms.

"I'm sure something can be arranged," he murmured.

Four days later, Eva found herself ringing Griffin's doorbell. She and Griffin had agreed to meet at his place to discuss wedding details.

She'd come straight from a business dinner with

a potential client, and was dressed in a red V-neck top and knee-length beige skirt.

When Griffin opened the door, she swallowed. He was dressed casually in black jeans and a dark blue open-collar shirt and looked incredibly sexy.

"Come on in," he said easily.

She wet her lips as she followed him. "Sorry, I'm late. Dinner went on longer than expected."

"No problem. I had a quick meal and was just sitting back with some business reports."

He began to lead the way through the house, but then stopped unexpectedly at the open doorway of the pool room.

"Do you play?" he asked.

Did she play? Of course, she did. She'd grown up with a pool table in the house, and she'd learned from the best: Marcus Tremont.

She'd just been sure over the years never to be drawn into a game against Griffin. A head-to-head competition with him over green felt and cue sticks should have been a battle fraught with meaning for her. When he'd visited the Tremont estate, and she'd unfortunately been present as well, she'd left him to play against her father.

"Sometimes," she said noncommittally.

A smile played at his lips as he walked over to a

wall-mounted cue rack. "Come on. Choose your weapon."

She hesitated. "I thought we were going to discuss wedding details."

He arched a brow. "We are. Over a game of pool. All right with you?"

She shrugged. "Okay."

Who was she to walk away now he'd thrown down the gauntlet? There was a part of her that had been waiting for years to beat his sorry rear end.

She walked over to him and chose one of the shorter cue sticks from the rack. "I hope this game isn't boring for you."

"I'll give you some pointers, if you need them," he offered, choosing a stick himself.

She smiled demurely, her eyes lowered. "Thank you."

She felt like a hustler, but wasn't everything fair in love and war? Troublingly, though, things were getting murky as to whether this was *love* or *war.*

He packed the balls in the rack, and when he was done, he said, "Do you want to break?"

"Sure, why not?"

She came around and bent over her cue stick.

She felt him study her intently, and while she knew her body alignment was perfect, she was very aware that her breasts had dropped forward, her cleavage on display at the neck of her crimson V-neck knit top.

Still, she kept her concentration and broke cleanly. The number three ball dropped into a corner pocket.

"I'll take it," she said.

She'd have to sink the rest of the solid colors, while he'd have the higher numbered striped balls.

She studied the table.

"Four ball into the corner pocket," she called, proceeding to sink the ball.

She saw Griffin's eyes narrow. Clearly he'd caught on that she was going to be a worthy competitor.

Next, she hit a combination shot, sending the cue ball into the six ball, which in turn hit the two ball into the side pocket.

When she missed on the following shot, she straightened and smiled. "Your turn."

He looked at her with wry amusement. "I was starting to think that the game would be over before I had a chance to make a shot."

"Beginner's luck," she said blithely.

"Best of three," he parried.

She shrugged. One game, two games, or three. It didn't matter. Now that she'd taken him on, she was determined to play this out.

Griffin made his first shot. Then he tried a difficult combination and sank cleanly.

He leveled her with a smile that was pure gamesman.

She set her teeth, but then acknowledged she'd hardly expected him to be a pushover.

"This match will be over before we get to any wedding details," she pointed out.

"So talk."

"I'd like to have the wedding at my parents' house and keep things small," she said, knowing the location would help her feel comfortable with her crazy decision to go off a cliff and marry Griffin.

"Fine. But if we're not eloping, I want us to get married quickly. A few weeks. Since we're using your parents' house, it shouldn't be a problem."

"Okay. That makes sense. We're trying to beat my biological clock, after all," she returned, reminding them both of the reason for their marriage.

He gave her an inscrutable look.

She cleared her throat. "About a prenup…"

He smiled enigmatically. "No need. We're both independently wealthy."

Her eyes widened. "California is a community property state. Fifty-fifty on divorce. I could take you to the cleaners."

Now that she'd seen where he lived and had gleaned some more details about him from his friends and associates, she knew he was out of her league in terms of wealth. True, she wasn't poor, but Occasions by Design paled in comparison to his company.

And while she was an heiress, the day she'd *inherit* was probably a long way off. In the meantime, she had a respectable—but from his perspective, certainly not lavish—trust fund and her own hard-earned money.

He sank another ball. "It's a gamble I'm willing to take."

"Griffin…" Her tone held a note of caution.

She couldn't believe she was dissuading him from making *his* money vulnerable to *her.* And from his amused expression, she could tell he was thinking the same thing.

"So we have no prenup," he said. "Since I credit your father with getting my money train moving, I'm not too worried about it winding up in Tremont hands."

She gave up. If he wanted to gamble with his money, it was his business.

"Where will we live?" she tried.

He lifted a brow and looked around them. "Do you think this place is big enough for the both of us?"

She adored his house. She had the minute she'd seen it. "Okay. I'll rent my condo, and then think about selling it at the right moment."

"A woman after my own heart," he said with mock solemnity.

She knew he was joking, but a tingle went through her anyway.

Before she could say anything else, however, Griffin missed his next shot, and she was up.

As they played, the conversation veered toward mundane wedding details. They discussed the guest list, and decided on the officiant. Because both their calendars couldn't be cleared for an extended period on short notice, they decided to honeymoon for a few days only at Griffin's getaway in Napa Valley.

As the conversation about the wedding wound down, Griffin called his shot, and the thirteen ball slid into a corner pocket.

Her seven ball, the eight ball and the cue ball remained. Griffin had to sink only the eight ball with the white cue ball to win.

She'd gone head-to-head with Griffin, and it had been a close game. *She'd been in this to win, however.*

Eva closed her eyes. She couldn't watch Griffin make his shot.

"Seven ball and eight ball in the corner pocket."

Her eyes flew open. She didn't understand. Were they playing by rules she wasn't aware of?

She focused in time to see Griffin very deliberately sink her seven ball along with the eight ball.

He straightened, and gave her a slow, sexy smile. "I consider this a win-win situation."

She stared at him. "Why?"

He put down his cue, and came around the table toward her. He removed the cue stick from her limp grasp, and set it aside. "The art of a successful hustle is to get your opponents to bet the house and empty their pockets."

Her eyes widened.

The side of his mouth lifted. "Isn't that what you were trying to do?"

She felt herself flush. "I—"

"So I decided to oblige you. This has been burning a hole in my pocket since you walked in the door."

He pulled something from his pocket, and grasping her hand, slid a ring onto her third finger.

She stared down at the brilliant cushion-cut diamond set in a filigreed setting. It had to be at least four carats.

Her lips parted. *Oh, my…*

She suddenly, inexplicably, felt like crying.

She hadn't gotten a ring from Carter before she'd found out about his betrayal.

Griffin was obviously making a statement—in more ways than one.

Her gaze rose to his.

"If you don't like it, we can get you something else."

She cleared her throat. "It's…*thank you.*"

His eyes burned into hers, and her breath caught.

A moment later, his lips touched hers, and she melted into him, kissing him back with all the pent-up sexual desire that had been building between them since she'd walked into his house.

His lips trailed along her neck.

"Why didn't I ever know you played pool?" he muttered against her throat.

"I…I didn't ever want to play you," she said breathlessly. "Stakes too high."

"Oh, yeah," he returned, and a moment later, her back met the wall.

She'd never had an adrenaline rush like this. She closed her eyes, and gave herself up to the passion between them.

He shoved her underwear down, and she heard the hiss of his zipper.

"Wrap your legs around me, kitten," he said roughly.

She complied, and he hiked her up, helping her while he kissed her deeply.

She was slick and wet, and they both groaned as he entered her.

The coming together was quick, hard and feverish. Within minutes, they found oblivion together.

Nine

Eva stared at herself in the full-length mirror in the bridal shop fitting area. The ivory wedding gown she wore was as slinky as a floor-length negligee.

She stood on a platform, and she turned to eye her back in the dressing area's three-way mirror.

The gown's almost backless style showcased a smooth expanse of skin from her neck down to the indentation of her waist.

The wedding was only two weeks away, and given the short notice, a custom-ordered gown had been out of the question.

"You look beautiful, Eva," Beth said from

nearby, her reflection caught in the dressing room mirror.

"Thank you."

"Griffin will be knocked off his feet."

"And not by a San Francisco earthquake, either," she replied.

Beth gave a tinkling laugh. "Trust you to create your own earthquake."

She'd felt the earth move all right, Eva thought. But it had had nothing to do with seismic shifts belowground. Instead she'd felt the world tilt right in Griffin's bed.

At the thought of returning there, a tremor took hold of her.

"The gown does flatter you spectacularly well, dear," her mother said, speaking up from where she was sitting in a nearby upholstered chair.

"Thanks, Mom."

Her mother gave a sudden watery smile. "My baby is getting married."

"Oh, Mom."

Her mother waved a hand away. "Your father is happy."

Happy? Try *ecstatic,* Eva wanted to say.

When she and Griffin had announced to her parents days ago that they planned to wed, her father's face had been wreathed in smiles.

It had been a far cry from her father's reaction to her plans to marry Carter. On top of it all, her father had acted as if the element of convenience to her marriage to Griffin was just an insignificant detail.

"If I hadn't known Griffin such a long time," her mother said now, "I would have worried about your decision to marry him this fast."

Eva reflected that at least one of her parents was willing to be levelheaded about her marriage to Griffin.

Still, she knew she owed it to her mother to be reassuring. Now that she'd made up her mind to marry Griffin, she was determined to see it through, and she didn't want her mother to have a moment of concern.

"In a way, it's not fast at all," she said lightly. "I've known Griffin just as many years as you and Dad have."

She kept more equivocal thoughts to herself as she turned back around and stared at herself in the mirror.

Who was this woman who had agreed to walk down the aisle in a couple of weeks? *And what had she done?*

Since she'd agreed to marry Griffin last week, her life had been in tumult. She was full of jittery excitement and quivering anticipation—alternating with moments of pure panic.

Griffin overwhelmed her. Ever since they'd slept

together after the party at his Pacific Heights mansion, she'd felt like herself but not herself. Certainly she was acting uncharacteristically, as witnessed by her decision to accept his proposal.

And though she'd once never have guessed it, Griffin had proven to be the most exciting, inventive bed partner she'd ever had.

Now, the thought of more of those nights stretching endlessly before her brought her body to tingly awareness.

"You know," Beth observed, "I've always thought Griffin was attracted by your acerbic wit."

"Thanks," Eva responded dryly. "I hope you're right because he's about to get a lot more of it."

Beth winked. "Planning to spice up the bedroom, hmm?"

Eva shot a glance at her mother, who was busy extracting a tissue from her purse and appeared not to have heard.

If only Beth knew, Eva thought to herself.

Beneath Griffin's cool, polished veneer lurked a heated passion that was capable of melting all her defenses.

"Congratulations again!" Marcus said heartily, extending a snifter of amber liquid.

Griffin accepted the glass from the older man.

He'd just arrived at the Tremont estate. After being shown in by the housekeeper, he'd waited in the front hall while she'd gone in search of one of the Tremonts.

Evidently, while the housekeeper had returned to inform him that he could join Marcus in the living room, the older man had taken the opportunity to pour them both drinks.

Griffin looked down at the glass in his hand and then back up at Marcus. "Brandy?"

"Only the best," Marcus responded, lifting his own glass. "To your good health, a long marriage and many grandchildren."

Griffin took an obligatory sip. "If Eva heard you talking that way, she wouldn't be pleased."

Marcus winked. "That's why I saved that little toast for this occasion."

Griffin looked around. "Where is Eva, by the way? We were supposed to meet here for dinner and to discuss more wedding details."

"Still out with her mother," Marcus responded. "Finding a dress or some other wedding paraphernalia."

Griffin felt disappointment hit him. He'd been hoping Eva would be at the house before him. In fact, in the past two weeks, he'd had an itch to see her, be around her and touch her all the time.

Marcus slapped him on the back. "I don't know exactly how you did it, Grif. I admit I thought everything was lost," the older man said, "but you got rid of Carter, and convinced Eva to marry you, all in record time!"

Griffin felt a prick to his conscience at the older man's words. He hadn't just manipulated Eva for his own ends.

"Eva wants a baby."

"Yes, I know," Marcus shot back, "but better you than Carter as the father of my grandchild."

"I just want it understood."

He wanted it understood he was in this marriage for Eva's sake. *And for the sake of his now insatiable need for her.*

Marcus, however, seemed oblivious to his thoughts. He sipped his brandy, and his expression became thoughtful.

"I'd like to offer you a piece of Tremont REH," the older man said. "You've certainly earned it. You can take the lion's share of the credit for REH's recent successes."

Griffin's lips quirked up on one side. "My answer's the same as last time. No."

He and Marcus had been down this road at least two or three times.

"I'm marrying Eva because I want to," he said,

his expression bland. "She's not just some pawn in a bigger game."

After a moment, the older man cracked a smile, as if something had been settled in his mind. "That's all I needed to know."

They both tossed back some of their brandy.

Marcus gave him a wry look. "You know, Eva is—"

Perfect. Sexy as hell. The missing jigsaw piece to his puzzle.

"—strong willed. It'll take a strong man to be married to her."

"Since I've endured you as chairman of my board of directors," Griffin replied sardonically, "I should be up to the job."

Marcus roared with laughter.

"It's what I'm counting on," the older man responded, a twinkle in his eye.

Griffin felt a tightening in his gut as the music struck up. It had been a crazy three weeks since Eva had accepted his proposal, and now here they were.

From behind French doors, Eva appeared on the large veranda that ran behind the Tremont mansion.

Griffin couldn't take his eyes off her as she started down the makeshift aisle created by folding chairs, her arm linked through her father's, a tight, round bouquet of calla lilies caught in one hand.

Her simple, spaghetti-strap gown flowed over her curves, hugging in just the right places. Her upswept hair was dotted with white flower buds.

Though he was dressed in a charcoal suit paired with an ivory silk tie, he felt like a rough-hewn escort for such elegant perfection.

When Eva reached him, she turned to hand her bouquet for safekeeping to Beth Harding, who was sitting nearby.

As he took in the back of her gown—or rather the lack thereof—he fought the urge to scoop her up and whisk her away to start their honeymoon right then.

The ceremony was brief, highlighted with music from a string quartet. They exchanged simple platinum bands inscribed with the date. And before he knew it, it was time to kiss the bride.

He didn't give Eva a chance to back away. He tilted up her chin and placed his lips firmly over hers, intending to give her a kiss full of sensual promise—slow, deep and thorough.

Instead he was pulled under her spell. Her lips parted beneath his, and with a sigh, she melted into him. Her soft curves molded to him and her arm slid around his neck.

He felt his desire roar to life.

Hearing the guests begin to laugh and applaud, however, he reluctantly lifted his head and stepped away.

Eva looked a little flustered, but she smiled at their audience and retrieved her bouquet from Beth.

As he walked down the aisle with her, her body brushed against his. He was tempted to keep going beyond the French doors that led into the Tremonts' living room, straight through the mansion, into his car and on to their honeymoon destination, where he could ravish her at his cottage in wine country.

Instead, once inside, he fixed a smile on his face as they posed for pictures and accepted the congratulations of their assembled family and friends.

Afterward, Eva left his side to go freshen up, only to stop to speak with the Hardings.

As he watched the late-afternoon sun bathe her in an ethereal light, Griffin felt an enormous sense of satisfaction wash over him.

Eva was now his wife. He'd meant to have her and he'd gotten her.

"Contemplating your newly shackled state?"

He turned to look at his brother, who'd approached while he'd been focused on Eva.

"Shackled? Is that what it's called?" he murmured.

If he was *tied,* then he was handcuffed to a desirable siren who was dynamite in bed.

It was a torture he could live with.

He shook his head as one of the waitstaff invited him to sample from a tray of salmon and lox hors d'oeuvres. The wedding reception was being catered by one of the companies regularly employed by Occasions by Design.

"I'll admit to being surprised," Josh went on. "It wouldn't have been a bad bet to wager you were a confirmed bachelor. Since you already got a double dose of responsibility with me and Monica, I figured you wouldn't be out looking for more anytime soon."

"Eva's hardly a responsibility," he returned, somewhat surprised by how readily the response came to him. "She's an independent woman who owns and runs her own company."

One who'd probably hit his brother over the head with a tray of hors d'oeuvres if she ever heard him calling her *a responsibility.*

The image made Griffin smile.

"Yes," Josh continued thoughtfully, "but she's also a woman who's desperate to have a kid. And where there are kids, there are responsibilities."

Griffin reflected that, as far as his siblings were concerned, his and Eva's was a conventional marriage, but with an element of convenience on both sides: her desire for a baby, and his willingness to marry and have a child that would inherit both REH and Evkit.

He certainly hadn't gone into details about his role in bringing about an end to Eva and Carter's couple-dom. Still, he knew his siblings would be curious, particularly since Monica was aware Eva had been dating Carter until recently.

"Frankly Monica and I had been hoping for something more salacious," Josh joked. "It would have been a lot more interesting if you'd married Eva after beating out another guy. Anything to spice up your image."

His brother didn't know how close to home he was hitting.

"Sorry to disappoint," he quipped. "But hey, have you thought about life as a comic?"

Josh grinned, and then held up his hands. "What? And waste these surgeon's hands? Or worse, risk having some irate comedy club patron break a finger or two?"

Griffin arched a brow. "I recall saving those million-dollar hands of yours from the *irate* brother of your high school girlfriend."

"Face it, Grif," Josh parried, unwilling to back down. "You're just the responsible type. It's time to quit running from your nature. You see a damsel in distress, you have to jump in."

"Shut up, Josh," he grumbled.

His brother cocked his head. "You know, Monica

and I initially had some doubts when you told us you were planning to wed Eva Tremont."

"I figured you would."

"Monica was worried you've been at loose ends lately."

Griffin shrugged. "Maybe I thought it was time to settle down like the two of you have."

He tossed off the explanation, but his brother regarded him keenly.

"Yeah," Josh said, "but it helps when it's the right woman."

He and Josh looked across the room at Eva.

"At least she's not a pushover for your arrogant rear end," his brother remarked.

"Thanks," Griffin grumbled. "Your vote of confidence overwhelms me."

Josh grinned. "On second thought, after seeing the wedding kiss, I don't think Monica and I have anything to worry about."

Mrs. Griffin Slater.

Eva was still getting used to the name on her tongue as they pulled up to Griffin's getaway home in Napa Valley.

They'd left her parents' estate as soon as the wedding reception was over, still in their wedding clothes.

Emerging from the car, she drank in the sight of Griffin's house.

It was a charming two-story structure with a red terra-cotta-tiled roof, whitewashed walls and distressed green shutters.

Griffin came up beside her. "Like it? I bought it a couple of years ago."

She glanced at him. "I'm starting to realize you made a lot of changes a couple of years ago."

"Come on," he said smoothly. "I'll show you around. We'll unload the luggage from the car later."

Grasping the hem of her floor-length gown in one hand, she followed him over the gravelly driveway.

After Griffin opened the old-fashioned, planked-wood front door, Eva found herself stepping directly into the cottage's living room. It was made up in masculine colors of maroon and brown that would have made Marcus Tremont instantly comfortable. In fact, Eva could almost picture her father relaxing in the nail head recliner in one corner.

Following the living room was a dining room centered around a large wood table whose planks, she learned from Griffin, were stained alternately with red and white wine. The chairs were cast iron with woven leather seats and backs.

The kitchen rounded out the first floor. It had clay tile floors, Viking appliances and old-fashioned country cupboards. And, of course, a large wine rack. Copper pots hung from a ceiling rack and glazed ceramics adorned various shelves.

Outside, visible through sliding doors, was a deck and an outdoor kitchen.

As they retraced their steps, Eva reflected that the lower level of the house displayed a very Napa style.

When they reached the front of the house again, they ascended an old-fashioned staircase with an ornate wood balustrade.

"There are three bedrooms up here, each with its own bath," Griffin said.

"Do you often have houseguests?"

He tossed her a look. "No, unless you count a couple of visits from my siblings, but I've only owned the house for a couple of years. Of course, if you'd like to entertain here, I wouldn't be opposed to it."

She'd *love* to entertain here, Eva thought. Griffin's house was made for entertaining.

After they'd peeked into the two guest suites, Griffin led her through the double doors to the master suite at the end of the hall.

Immediately she got an impression of bold splashes of color. The walls were painted a forest-green, but what really caught he attention was the king-size bed with wine-red satin bedding and an ornately carved dark wood headboard.

It would be like making love in an arbor, or, she thought, as her eyes went to the view of verdant hills visible from the large paned-glass windows, among vineyards and grape-stained ground.

She became acutely aware of Griffin standing next to her.

"Well? What do you think?" he asked.

"Do you arrange all your tours so they end up in your bedroom?" she said, her flippant tone belying her sudden tension.

Griffin smiled slowly. "You noticed."

She felt the air grow thick. "Yes."

"Most women would catch on to the maneuver fast," Griffin murmured. "And since you're not stupid or unobservant, I've got to assume you're here because you want to be."

She tilted her head. "*Maybe.* Have you tried this with many women?"

"You're the only one who's fallen for the ploy."

He gave her a wolfish look, and she pretended to look offended.

When she would have moved away, however, he slipped his arm around her waist, drawing her to him.

The contact was electric.

He searched her face, his expression suddenly solemn. "You're also the only woman I've tried the tactic with."

Ten

He wanted to make love to her so badly, Griffin felt as if he might come out of his skin. "I've always thought only a tough man could take you on."

She wet her lips. "Think you're up to the job?"

"I'm betting the house on it."

He massaged the muscles of her lower back and felt her relax, even as her nipples tightened and pressed into him through the fabric of her gown. He was getting more aroused by the second with her in his arms.

"I have to warn you," she said huskily.

He felt the urge to laugh at her need to warn him.

He *would have* laughed if he hadn't been feeling like a live wire conducting currents of desire.

"Mmm?" His eyes focused on her moist, delectable mouth, but he was also attuned to other alluring parts of her. "What do I need to be warned about?"

"I've got to warn you that I *never* wanted to marry someone like my father. Even before Carter."

"And I'm like your father?" he questioned idly, his hands going to the zipper at the back of her dress.

He'd been waiting for hours to unmask her curves. He wanted to explore them without any barrier.

Eva nodded. "You put work first. I almost married Carter because he paid attention."

"Believe me," he joked, "you've got my *complete* attention."

As if to drive the point home, he nuzzled her neck, sliding down the zipper of her dress.

He had to have her *now.* Before he exploded.

Why were they talking about *inattention* when his problem was he couldn't get her off his mind?

She'd cluttered his brain so much he had trouble concentrating on anything else.

"I just want you to know where I stand," she said throatily.

When her dress slithered to the floor, she stood clad only in white lacy panties and sky-high heels— just delicious curves and endless legs.

His mouth went dry, and he swallowed. "I'd say where you stand at the moment is nearly naked in my arms."

"Be serious."

She wanted him to be serious? He'd never been more serious about anything. Right now, he was single-mindedly focused on fitting himself to her.

Still, he decided to play along as his hands skimmed her curves. "I have no illusions. You're after my millions of sperm."

"I'm glad you're okay with it," she breathed.

"Well, it's tough being up against several hundred million little guys and coming out ahead."

They were doing a dangerous dance, but he was ready for her. *More than ready.* The thought of impregnating Eva made him rock hard.

He planted moist kisses along her jaw, and then his hands grasped her pert rear end and brought her flush against him.

Her eyes darkened, and then she pulled his head down to hers.

The kiss was scorching. Their tongues met, feinted and parried.

His fingers tunneled into her hair, loosening pins, so he could angle her head and master the kiss.

He wanted to be consumed by the heat. He

wanted the essence of her to surround him, and he wanted to lose himself inside her.

When he finally lifted his head, he was breathing hard.

He noted that Eva looked flushed, her mouth puffy and her eyes glittering.

"I've got to have you," he said harshly.

Instead of answering him, she let her hands caress his bulge, a dreamy half smile curving her lips.

He groaned, and then swore. Her touch was exquisite and made him want her all the more.

He wanted to make this last. He wanted to draw out the moment until they were both balanced on the precipice, teetering at the edge of almost unbearable exquisite sensation, where one more caress might send them over. Still, the urge to be inside her and find sweet release was overwhelming.

He pushed her hands aside urgently, and she fell back onto the bed, her sandals hitting the floor.

"You're driving me crazy," he growled.

As she raised herself up on her elbows, he began to strip.

She smiled up at him, seemingly drunk on the insane passion between them.

When he tossed aside his briefs, she said, "I'm off the pill."

The side of his mouth quirked up. "Great. I'll

pass along the info to the two hundred million or so interested parties."

She made a sound that came out halfway between a laugh and gasp.

He reached out and ran his hand down her leg—along her thigh to the indentation of her knee and then down her calf.

Raising her leg, he kissed the inside of her ankle, then the delicate skin of her arch. His other hand smoothed toward the hidden recesses covered by her dark curls.

Eva squirmed. "Griffin!"

This was what he'd fantasized about—Eva, stripped of her protective layers and wanting him.

"Yes, say my name," he said, reaching forward and stripping the panties from her. He wanted her to remember *who* was making her feel this good.

Tossing her underwear aside, he stretched out next to her on the bed and pulled her on top of him.

She straddled him, and because her hair had come loose from its pins, stray strands tickled his face.

Her topaz gaze held his as, guided by his hands on her hips, she sank down on him, inch by delicious inch. When he was fully embedded inside her, they both expelled a breath of satisfaction.

He moved then, thrusting, and she parried, taking up the rhythm.

She arched her back, her midnight hair a glorious inky silhouette for her smooth, ivory skin.

Higher and higher they went, scaling to the peak, Eva's moans mingling with his own harsh breaths.

His focus narrowed on his driving need, but he was determined to hold back until he made it good for her.

When he eventually felt Eva's climax coming on in long, undulating waves, he took pleasure in having her come undone for him.

Only then did he groan and he let himself go, triggering an explosive release that sent him into the vortex.

"Hello?" Griffin called, closing the front door behind him.

It was Wednesday, and he'd decided to come home early from work to surprise Eva.

Okay, who was he kidding?

He was home early because he needed to see Eva—be with her.

In the couple of weeks since they'd come back from their brief honeymoon, he found his mind regularly drifting off to erotic fantasies. He couldn't get her out of his mind, and he didn't want to.

He set his leather briefcase down on the console table in the entry hall, and loosened his tie.

"Hello?" he said again.

Maybe Eva was out. Working, shopping or seeing a friend. Disappointment seeped through him. He'd grown used to having someone to come home to.

The house in Pacific Heights had come to life for him since Eva had moved in.

Upon their return from their honeymoon weekend in Napa, movers had made short work of moving Eva's key possessions from her Russian Hill condo to his—no, *their*—mansion in Pacific Heights.

As soon as Eva decided what she wanted to do with her remaining furniture, he'd deal with renting her condo.

He was in no hurry. He'd rushed her to the altar, but he could be patient as they adjusted to being married.

Now, the sound of distant music reached him, and abruptly, he went still and listened.

He could just make out the notes of some classical arrangement.

He looked up the grand curving stairwell to the floor above. The music seemed to be coming from the second level.

Undoing his tie completely, he climbed the stairs two at a time.

At the landing, he let his gaze sweep the series of closed doors. Then after a moment, he strode purposely toward one of the unfurnished guest bedrooms.

After he turned the knob and pushed the door open, surprise rooted him to the spot.

Eva kicked and dipped and let her arms fan out in the empty room, oblivious to his presence. She was clad in a black leotard and matching ballet slippers, her hair in a ponytail.

An iPod sat in a corner, set in a doughnut-shaped speaker base. Music—ethereal and pretty—drifted through the room as Eva rose en pointe, her arms gracefully outstretched.

Bemused, Griffin held his breath. He knew she'd taken ballet lessons for years, but he hadn't had a clue she'd continued to dance.

Watching her, he felt his body tighten and stir. She appeared delicate and airy as she moved.

When she did a pirouette, he could see the exact moment she caught sight of him.

Her eyes widened, but there was no break in her spin, and seconds later, she dipped as the music died away.

Seconds later, she straightened, her arms falling to her sides, and he started to clap.

"Hi," she said, her heart visibly pounding from her exertions.

The corners of his mouth lifted. "Hi yourself. I didn't know you still danced," he said.

"Only at home, and for fun."

"Any other accomplishments I should be aware of?"

She lifted a shoulder negligently. "Ballet and pool... and, oh yes, party planning. That's the extent of it."

His lips quirked up again. "Impressive."

She blew a breath, causing the tendrils of hair around her face to lift and fall. "When I started Occasions by Design, I'd take any account that walked in the door." She looked him in the eye, as if daring him to laugh. "I wound up doing a lot of kids' parties—where I'd dress up as a ballerina."

"That must have been some interesting way to start a company," he said, keeping a poker face.

"I didn't mind. I always wanted a big family, and it was one way to be around lots of kids."

This time, he let himself smile. "I can just picture you in the whole pink tulle outfit."

It dawned on him that Eva must really have an affinity for kids. The possibility of infertility must have hit her hard. At the same time, he realized the thought of having *lots* of kids with her didn't bother him in the least.

"Yes, it was pink tulle," Eva confirmed. "I could have been a cake topper."

He laughed. "Now, about this big family idea—"

She pinked.

"Is your longing for a big family because—"

"—I was an only child?" She shook her head. "I don't want you to think I was unhappy, because my parents doted on me. But when I was at friends' houses, I could see how much fun they had with their siblings."

He understood the truth of the last statement. "After my parents died, it was good to have my siblings around."

Eva looked surprised. "You didn't think of taking care of your siblings a burden?"

Griffin guessed there was a good chance someone—maybe Marcus, or perhaps Monica—had provided Eva with some details about his life in the years following his parents' death.

He pulled off his tie with one hand. "There were times when I thought of it as a burden," he admitted, "but now I also appreciate how lucky I was."

"I like your brother and sister," she remarked. "They're nice people."

"But I'm not?" he teased, and then watched her flush.

He was beginning to enjoy coaxing adorable flustered reactions out of her.

"You're home early," she commented, instead of answering him directly.

"Yes." They were in this marriage to get her

pregnant, so how did he announce to his wife that he was running home because he couldn't stand being away from her?

She glanced around them. "I didn't mean to commandeer this room for my ballet escapes."

"It's your house, too," he responded as their eyes met. "And I don't mind."

He really didn't mind. He could get used to coming home to his wife dancing for him. *Definitely*.

"How about we make this room the ballet room?" he suggested. "It's empty, and I can't think of a better way to use it."

She looked doubtful. "You don't mind?"

He smiled seductively. "No—especially if I get to enjoy private dance performances."

"I think that can be arranged," she responded huskily.

He moved toward her. "Good."

He drew her into his arms, and she sighed just before his lips met hers.

And then there was no more talking for a long time as he showed her just how much of a patron of dance he could be.

Griffin woke feeling damn good.

The bedroom was still dark, however, and a

quick check of the bedside clock revealed it was just after midnight.

Looking over at the space next him, he realized Eva wasn't in bed. He frowned, and then figured she must have woken up and gone to get a drink or something.

He let his head sink against his pillow again, and his mind wander over the events of the previous evening.

From the newly designated ballet room, he'd carried Eva back to their bedroom, where they'd made love sprawled across their bed.

Afterward, they'd had fun preparing dinner. Since they'd married, he'd discovered that Eva's party planning skills had spilled over into ancillary areas, and she was a wiz at whipping together diverse ingredients into a quick meal.

She'd quickly prepared a chicken carbonara dish, while he'd tossed a baby spinach salad with almond slivers and orange slices.

After dinner, they'd cleaned up together, falling into a routine that had taken root between them in the brief time they'd been married. And afterward, they'd lingered for hours over coffee in the living room while soft jazz played in the background.

As on many previous nights, their conversation had ranged far and wide. He'd discovered that while he liked jazz, her musical taste tended toward classical tunes that were ballet standards. But they were both fans of the San Francisco 49ers and, it turned out, hiking and mountain biking.

Eva had claimed hiking kept her legs in ballet shape, and he'd claimed to like the shape of her legs. She'd hit him with a sofa pillow, and to his satisfaction, they'd wound up horizontal for the second time that evening.

Now, he wondered why Eva hadn't come back to bed yet. Rising from the bed, he padded to the door, clad only in his boxers.

When he got downstairs, he headed to the kitchen. On the way, however, a noise from his study made him stop.

He walked to the study door and pushed it open a few inches. Light flickered inside the room, as if someone were watching TV.

He pushed the door open even farther and noticed Eva sitting at his desk, her back to him, staring at his computer screen.

He stopped dead when he realized what she was watching.

Ron's DVD of Carter's sex romp.

There was no sound from the computer, so the volume must have been turned off on the speakers.

Over Eva's shoulders, Griffin watched as Carter

and his lover emerged from their car and straightened their clothes.

After a moment, however, Griffin decided to back away from the door and turn around. His feet took him in the direction of the stairs. He was going back to bed. *As if he could sleep.*

Damn it.

Eva must have found Ron's evidence in the drawer of his desk. He wished now he hadn't been so careless about where he put it. He should have left the stuff at the office, except he hadn't wanted anyone accidentally discovering it.

Of course, after Eva had moved in, *she'd* discovered Ron's damned collection. He belatedly acknowledged he would have been better off destroying the evidence weeks ago.

Griffin felt his gut twist.

If Eva had gone to the trouble of locating Ron's evidence, it could only mean she hadn't entirely forgotten about Carter.

He told himself there wasn't anything surprising about Eva still being preoccupied with Carter. It hadn't been so long, after all, since her relationship with Carter had ended, and *he'd* rushed her to the altar.

Because he wanted her so damn badly.

Still, he wondered whether there was even more to Eva's curiosity. Maybe she was having doubts about kicking Newell out of her life without a second chance.

Sure, the past few weeks had proven—to him, at least—that he and Eva were fantastic together.

But Eva could have been having doubts about their marriage.

Eleven

Eva stared at her doctor in shock.

It was a sunny late Thursday afternoon, and she'd come in for what she'd thought was a routine gynecological exam. Instead she'd gotten a grenade in her lap.

She'd been a patient of Leticia Bainbridge for almost a decade. Her doctor was an energetic woman in her early fifties who was married with two teenage children.

She watched Dr. Bainbridge's mouth move, but couldn't process the words. They were drowned out by the death knell she heard sounding on her fertility.

"Uterine fibroids…"

"—wait and see…"

"Surgery…embolization… Possible myomectomy."

A routine exam had led her doctor to note that her uterus was somewhat enlarged.

She'd been moved to another exam room, where the presence of growths within her uterus had been confirmed by an abdominal ultrasound.

"How could this happen without my knowing it?" she asked. "I haven't experienced any pain."

"Not all women have symptoms," Dr. Bainbridge said kindly.

"You haven't mentioned hysterectomy," she forced herself to say.

She felt unsteady, shaky.

If they removed her uterus, any chance she had of getting pregnant would be gone.

"There are options aside from hysterectomy these days," Dr. Bainbridge said. "We could try to shrink the fibroids through radiology, or perform a myomectomy, which, in your case, may ultimately be our best bet. A myomectomy would involve removing the fibroids surgically while leaving the uterus intact."

"Still," Eva persisted, "this means my chances of getting pregnant are greatly reduced, doesn't it?"

She almost couldn't stand to be confronted with

the bald-faced truth. She couldn't afford another strike against her. It was bad enough her egg supply was sinking fast. By the day, in fact.

"It may make it a harder for you to conceive, yes," Dr. Bainbridge said carefully.

Harder? Eva heard the word echo in her mind. Just how much was *harder* before her chances became *nil?* The average couple had only a twenty percent chance or so of conceiving in any given month.

She'd become acquainted with fertility statistics since becoming aware of her own rapidly ticking biological clock. She'd made it her business to know the stats and the facts.

All at once, she wanted to cry.

Instead she heard herself say hollowly, "Thank you for explaining the diagnosis to me."

Her mind went to Griffin, and his words came back to her, haunting in retrospect. *You're after my millions of sperm.*

Their marriage was based on a straightforward agreement to conceive a child. Now that conceiving a child was more elusive than ever, where did that leave her marriage?

With sudden startling clarity, she realized that, somewhere along the way, the goal of having *a child* had been replaced by the dream of having *Griffin's child.*

She was in love with her husband.

And the realization, instead of resulting in a burst of joy, as it would have just an hour ago, caused her to panic.

"I'll leave you to get dressed," Dr. Bainbridge said. "I'm sure we'll be speaking more in the coming days and weeks."

When the doctor had left the room, Eva hopped down from the examining table, removed the gown she wore and started to dress.

She expected her hands to be shaking, but the tumult was all inside her.

These past few weeks with Griffin had been some of the best of her life. It felt as if she'd finally been living in full color.

Their lives had seamlessly merged—more effortlessly than she could have imagined. But while they'd become comfortable with each other, their sex life had remained in hyperdrive.

She heated at the memories. They'd had sex in every position imaginable, and then some she hadn't even given thought to. Griffin, however, apparently *had*.

Her mind drifted back to a particularly steamy encounter they'd had last week, after he'd discovered her practicing ballet in one of the unfurnished bedrooms.

Later that night, while she'd watched Griffin sleep, his face relaxed and his chest rising and falling evenly, she'd acknowledged that her feelings for him were beginning to get muddied.

He'd been joking about being a designated sperm donor, but the reality was he was getting under her skin.

Troubled and restless, she'd gotten out of bed. She'd meant to head to the kitchen for a glass of milk, but instead, she'd found herself pausing outside the door to Griffin's study.

Without really knowing what she intended to do, she'd entered and turned on his computer. After idly surfing the Internet for several minutes, she'd opened one of Griffin's desk drawers.

Immediately, she'd spotted the DVD that she'd stumbled across earlier in the week, when she'd gone looking for a pad of paper to use during a phone call with a potential client. The DVD had been marked with Carter's name, and had been impossible to miss.

This second time, she hadn't hesitated. In the middle of the night, she'd popped the DVD into Griffin's computer and watched.

And she'd felt…absolutely nothing.

Now, she stared at the examining room's white wall.

Griffin was her present.

Her lover. Her husband. The man she loved.

It was hard to think of being married to him while she loved him desperately and he saw her as a *convenience.* It was worse, however, to think of doing so while she tried vainly for years to get pregnant.

With a growing sense of dread, she realized she'd have to tell Griffin about the doctor's diagnosis and give him an out.

Even at the cost of her heart.

When she arrived home an hour later, Griffin was there to meet her as she came in the door.

"You're here on the early side," she remarked.

She'd hoped to have more time to prepare for what she had to say, but she conceded it probably would have just prolonged the agony.

Griffin gave her a quick kiss on the lips. "I'm glad you're back." His eyes twinkled. "I had an epiphany at work."

He paused, as if expecting her to guess.

When she just looked at him mutely, his lips quirked.

"Belly dancing," he said.

She looked at him inquiringly, and his smile widened.

"I had this idea that you could take your dancing

skills in a whole new direction. Knowing what ballet does for our sex life, just think of what belly dancing will do."

She looked at him archly, and he affected an expression of mock solemnity.

"Purely in the interest of getting you pregnant, of course," he said.

"Of course," she echoed.

She knew he was joking, but the reminder of the purpose behind their marriage made her heart lurch.

Griffin winked. "Come on back to the kitchen, and I'll pour you a drink. Something nonalcoholic in case we already got started on the baby making."

Her heart lurched again.

He took a step toward the back of the house. "Tell me about your day. How was your visit to the doctor?"

She steeled herself. "Some unexpected news, actually. There's another stumbling block to my getting pregnant."

Griffin turned back toward her, and she watched him go still.

"Meaning?"

She took a deep breath. "I mean, I've been diagnosed with uterine fibroids. Many women get them, but in my case, it looks like surgery is a possibility, especially if I want to hang on to my fertility."

She watched Griffin frown and bit her lip. "It's

impossible to say how easily I'll be able to get pregnant after any procedure," she said. "And, as we both know, my chances of getting pregnant weren't good to begin with."

Griffin blew a breath. "Aw, kitten, I'm sorry."

She attempted a laugh. "I should be thankful there are options apart from a hysterectomy these days."

Griffin stepped toward her, but she raised a hand to stop him. If he touched her, she knew she would cry. Or worse, beg him to stay with her.

"I haven't finished," she said.

"There's more?"

He looked, Eva thought, as if he was wondering what else needed to be said after the nail in the coffin of her fertility.

"We married for a specific reason," she said. "Of course, now that that reason is gone, I won't expect to hold you to our arrangement."

Griffin's concerned expression melted away. "What do you mean? You said yourself, you don't know for sure whether you'll be able to get pregnant or not."

She forced herself to keep her expression neutral and her voice steady. "Exactly. I don't know for sure, but I know the odds are bad. There's no reason to stay together in the futile hope that one day I'll get pregnant."

Griffin's face became shuttered. "That's it? You're going to throw in the towel?"

"We married for a specific reason," she repeated.

"Yes, and now you're reneging on our bargain."

She felt her temper ignite. She was dealing with the end of her dreams of family *and* marriage, and he was talking to her about defaulting on a deal?

"Do you want to pass down Tremont REH so badly?" she said, giving him tit for tat. "If so, why don't you talk to my father? I'm sure it can be arranged, even without me."

Griffin's mouth thinned into an angry line. "You want out, you can have out."

"I'll stay at my condo while we iron out the details," she retorted.

He gave a terse nod, and then turned and strode down the hall.

A moment later, Eva heard a door slam.

Luckily, she thought miserably, she hadn't yet rented out or sold her town house. Now it would prove a welcome refuge while she got over Griffin.

If she could *ever* get over Griffin.

Damn it. Griffin nursed his brandy and wished he had Marcus's good stuff right now.

He'd heard Eva leave the house an hour ago, but he'd been holed up in his study.

He wasn't going to beg her to stay.

Even if the past few weeks had been some of the best of his life. Even if he'd formed a deeper connection to her than he'd had to any other woman.

She wanted out, she could have out.

He and his two hundred million or so sperm could take it like men, he thought with morbid humor.

He downed some more of the brandy and took empty solace in the warm path it traced to his gut.

He should have known his relationship with Eva would come to this kind of end. He'd gotten a hint last week, when he'd caught her watching Carter's sex tape. Ever since, he'd been ignoring the flicker of unease at the edge of his mind.

He cursed.

Things weren't over between them.

He'd seduce her, if he had to. Sex wasn't all there was between them, but it was a good start to getting her to understand how much more there was.

As much as he'd like children with Eva, what he really wanted—no, needed—was *her.*

"Get a divorce?"

Her father echoed her words, but the look on Marcus Tremont's face was nothing if not incredulous.

After arriving at her parents' mansion minutes

ago, Eva had located her parents having breakfast in the solarium.

Her father had been reading the newspaper, his eggs and toast set out before him. Her mother had been sipping tea and glancing through the mail set at the side of her breakfast plate.

They'd both looked bright and cheerful—that is, Eva thought, until she'd dropped her bombshell.

Eva wondered now how her parents hadn't spotted something was wrong the minute she'd walked into the room. She was exhausted, having had two sleepless nights.

After her conversation with Griffin two days ago, she'd gathered some of her personal belongings and headed to Russian Hill, where she'd been able to bawl her eyes out in the privacy of her old bedroom.

Her father now pushed back his chair and stood. "You can't get a divorce! You just got married, for God's sake! Or have you forgotten?"

"I haven't forgotten anything."

Sarcasm was usually a good indication of how agitated her father was, but she was too weary to rise to the bait.

Her father frowned. "Are you trying to compete with some of those starlets down in L.A. for the shortest marriage on record? *Two hours, thirty-seven seconds?*" he demanded. "If so, I'll remind you that I prefer to keep the Tremont name respectable."

"Oh, Marcus," her mother interrupted, rising from her seat. "Can't you see Eva's upset enough as it is?"

"Upset?" her father echoed, his voice ringing out. "This—" he stabbed a finger at his chest "—is what upset looks like."

Eva watched her mother come over to her, and in the next instant, she was enveloped in a comforting hug.

"I knew my happiness was too good to last," her father grumbled, and then lowered his eyebrows. "How could you possibly want to divorce Griffin?"

Eva reluctantly pulled away from her mother's embrace. "I'm glad you got around to asking the question."

Her father said with sudden suspicion, "He didn't cheat on you, did he?"

"No."

"Then what?"

What could she say? *I'm in love with Griffin but I can't stay married to him.*

It was too complicated to explain, so she sighed, and said wearily, "Does it really matter?"

"You *can't* divorce him," her father shot back. "I offered him a chunk of Tremont REH if he married you!"

A stunned silence followed her father's words.

"What?" she said incredulously. "I can't believe you!"

"Marcus!" her mother exclaimed, looking similarly shocked. "How could you do something like that?"

Her father looked at the two of them shrewdly. "They were some of my shares, Audrey."

Eva felt her temper ignite. "How does accepting ownership of Tremont REH in exchange for marrying me make Griffin any less of a gold digger than Carter?"

Her father's jaw set. "Griffin earned a stake in Tremont REH. He's been drawing a nominal salary as CEO, but his knack for investing is what put Tremont REH in the enviable position it's in today."

"Why not just offer him ownership in the company then?" she asked. "Why tie it to marrying me?"

"The company's name is *Tremont* REH for a good reason," her father said stubbornly, "and it's going to stay in Tremont hands as long as I draw breath."

She compressed her lips. "That's less likely now than ever."

"Of course it is! You're thinking of divorcing Griffin!"

She wondered what her father would say if she

told him about her visit to the doctor, but she figured she'd handed him enough of a shock already.

"How could you?" she demanded. "How could you bribe Griffin?"

Her gaze clashed with her father's, and then she turned on her heel and walked out of the house.

Rather than head home or to the office, however, she got in her car and headed back to the mansion in Pacific Heights.

Griffin was used to staring down opposing parties in business negotiations, but he hadn't yet had to deal with the full wrath of a Tremont.

Twelve

When she arrived in Pacific Heights an hour later, she had a full head of steam.

Eva let herself into the house with her key and slammed the door behind her.

She had only a few seconds to wait before Griffin appeared in the archway at the end of the entry hall that led to the back of the house.

She'd assumed he'd be home at this hour because it was Saturday and he didn't need to be at the office. He should also have had a chance to sleep in, but she noted peripherally that he looked a little beat.

"You miserable, rotten…" She trailed off, incoherent with rage.

He stared at her until the side of his mouth finally quirked up in sardonic amusement.

"Well, I have to give you credit for a refreshing response," he drawled. "*You* ask for a divorce, and *I'm* a miserable, rotten jerk."

"Thank you for supplying an appropriate name. Though *jerk* may be too good a word for you." She crossed her arms as he came closer. "How about liar? Or, wait—" she unfolded her arms and snapped her fingers, as if she'd just had a flash of insight "—how about gold digger, heiress hunter, or one of those other choice words that apply to Carter?"

Griffin's brows snapped together. "Don't put me in the same sentence as Newell."

"If the shoe fits," she returned sweetly.

"What are you talking about?"

She dropped her arms, growing impatient. "Come on, Griffin. My father told me."

"Told you what?"

"About how he offered you a sizable share of Tremont REH if you married me. Not content that our child—" she almost stumbled over the word "—would inherit the company, you decided to grab some for yourself, hmm?"

In a fit of anger two days ago, she'd suggested he work out something with her father for ownership of Tremont REH. Little had she known he'd already taken care of that small detail!

Emotions flitted across Griffin's face. It was a few moments before he answered.

"Bothered you, did it?" he said equably.

"What do you think?" she retorted. "How are you any different from Carter?"

"Because I didn't cheat on you?" he offered.

"Wrong answer," she said, his tongue-in-cheek response incensing her.

He cocked his head. "It bothered you that I might have been bribed to marry you? I wonder why, but I have a theory."

She gave a humorless laugh. "This should be good."

Hitting him with a serving tray or stabbing him with a dessert fork would be too good for him, she thought. Roasting him over a fondue flame, now there was an idea….

Griffin nodded thoughtfully and came closer, apparently unaware of how she nearly vibrated with anger.

"Want to hear my theory?" he said.

"I can't wait."

"You love me."

"Oh, right," she snapped even as her heart beat faster. "Do the words *hypocrite, liar* and *gold digger* mean nothing to you?"

"Yeah, but all those things are a drop in the bucket compared to the fact you love me and you think I betrayed you."

"You're forgetting I know all about betrayal," she responded coolly. "It no longer has any shock value for me."

He shook his head. "You didn't love Carter. But you do love me."

His arrogance took her breath away.

He regarded her perceptively. "What if I said there was never any payment from your father?"

"What?"

His eyes held hers. "I never received a stake in Tremont REH in return for marrying you."

"That's impossible," she said, holding on tenaciously to the facts as she knew them. "My father just said he offered you shares in Tremont REH."

"Offered, yes. *Accepted,* no."

She frantically replayed the conversation in her parents' mansion. Her father had said *offered.* It was a fine distinction.

She stared at Griffin. "He purposely misled me."

Griffin nodded, and her stomach plummeted. All at once, she felt deflated and teary.

"I'm sorry," she managed finally. "I can tell my fight isn't with you."

Blindly, she turned toward the door, but before she could take a step, Griffin grasped her arm.

"Eva, wait."

She looked at him in a blur. "Why? Why did he mislead me?"

A faint smile curved Griffin's lips. "I suspect because he thought it would send you straight back to confront me and we'd patch things up between us."

"A nice sentiment, but I'm still furious with him for even having made the *offer* of money."

"I don't think he ever intended it as a straightforward deal, with the Tremont shares conditional on my marrying you," Griffin countered. "I'm guessing he thought I could take some of the credit for Tremont REH's recent success—"

"Well, that's definitely true."

"—and offering the shares was more of an acknowledgment of past performance than, ah, let's say, future endeavors."

"You mean staying married to me, and with any luck, starting another generation of Tremonts?" she asked piercingly.

Griffin nodded, his thumb making circular motions on her skin where he still grasped her arm. "I think he was relieved when I turned him down."

Despite herself, she began to feel soothed.

Griffin smiled a little. "You have to admit, he had reason to be concerned after your brush with one fortune hunter."

She wavered. "I'd like to believe you."

"Believe it," Griffin said. "Marcus only mentioned handing over a part of the company to me *after* I told him I'd proposed to you. It was an after-the-fact offer on a done deal. He's offered me a stake in the company a number of times to ensure I'd stay on as CEO."

She looked at him in surprise. "He has?"

Griffin nodded. "And I've always turned him down."

As she tried to process all his revelations, a teasing glint entered Griffin's eyes.

"I didn't need that carrot to marry you," he said. "You've always been my favorite heiress."

Tears welled, and she blinked to hold them back.

"Ah, kitten."

She tried to break free of his grasp but he pulled her into his arms.

"No, let me go… I—I have to—"

"We'll adopt."

"No, no, that's not what you want. This marriage was just to get me pregnant."

"Maybe I'm not in it to get you pregnant. Maybe I'm not in it for a slice of Tremont REH."

"Well, you certainly don't need the m-money!" she choked out.

"Maybe I'm in this marriage because I love you."

"You can't," she cried, even as her heart flipped over.

Griffin laughed. "Are you going to stop telling me what I do and don't want?"

"You didn't even like me."

"The truth is I fought against wanting you for too long. When I almost lost you to Carter, I knew I had to take action."

"Did you?"

His expression became wry. "I figured if you were willing to settle for Carter, then you damn well could settle for me."

"You were going to let me divorce you."

"Not a chance," he contradicted. "Even if California does have no-fault divorce laws. I was going to fight for you. For us."

She sighed tremulously. "I wondered sometimes why I had such a hard time finding Mr. Right, even though I knew I had less time than most women to have kids. I think I cut it down to the wire and latched on to Carter because he happened to be around at the right moment."

"You've got that right," Griffin said dryly.

She gazed into his eyes. "Because all along it was

you, and I didn't want it to be you. You were my father's right-hand man for so long, and I *hated* it. I even had a secret name for you—Mr. Fix-It."

Griffin sighed but his expression was understanding. "Can we separate Tremont REH from us?"

She nodded and sniffled. "Now we can."

"Can you give me the words?" he asked, suddenly intent. "Because I need them."

He was strong, she realized. Strong enough to lay out his vulnerabilities—strong enough to give her courage.

She searched his expression, and felt a heartbreaking tenderness. "I love you, Griffin."

He expelled a pent-up breath and his lips quirked up. "For the record, I love you, too."

His hands dove into her hair, and he pulled her head back for a deep kiss. And he proceeded to demonstrate just how mutual her feelings were.

It was only much later, when they lay in a spent embrace in their bed upstairs, that either of them felt like doing much talking again.

"Ever wonder where the name Evkit comes from?" Griffin asked while she idly drew circles on his chest with her index finger.

"No, why?"

He smiled crookedly. "*Ev* from Eva, and *kit* for kitten."

She raised her head from his shoulder to look at him fully. *"No."*

He laughed at her tone of disbelief. "Like I said, you've always been my favorite heiress."

She punched his arm playfully. "I thought you didn't like me—or my job, for that matter. You were never at any of the parties that Occasions by Design planned."

"I purposely avoided them," he admitted, "because I didn't want to be tempted *by you*."

The man did wonders for her self-esteem, Eva thought in wonder, loving him all the more.

"Why didn't you just give in to temptation?" she said.

"After raising my siblings, I thought I was done with personal responsibilities for a lifetime, and getting involved with the boss's daughter would definitely have been complicated."

She propped herself on an elbow. "Monica filled me in a little recently about just how involved you were in raising her and Josh," she said. "Before that, as far as I could see, you were just my father's enforcer. The guy who looked down on me and my job."

"I enjoyed teasing you," he admitted. "I got an adrenaline rush out of butting heads with you. But ever since I saw you in action for Occasions by Design, I've known just how good you are at what you do."

She smiled, and then bit her lip. "About Tremont REH…"

He cocked a brow and bent an arm behind his head. "What about it? You grew up thinking you were in competition with Tremont REH for your father's attention. That explains your aversion to the real estate business."

She looked at him in surprise. "You knew?"

"It was hard to miss," he said dryly. "And I have to admit, I've come to realize Marcus probably didn't do himself any favors."

"For years, I thought you were just like my father."

"Have I ever made you feel like you're taking a backseat to something else?" he countered.

"No…"

It was true, she realized. In fact, Griffin had surprised her by how often he'd been home waiting for her. *Wanting to be with her.*

A teasing light entered his eyes. "Now about that Mr. Fix-It nickname…"

"Yes?"

With a deft move, he rolled her onto her back. "Let's try coming up with something else, shall we?"

"How about *Mr. Everything?*" she offered. "You know, as in *you are my everything.*"

"Nice try, kitten," he growled, "but I was thinking of something a little more manly."

She laughed, and then Griffin's lips met hers.

Epilogue

Griffin looked down at the infant daughter in his arms and felt his heart expand.

They'd come home from the hospital yesterday, and today they were hosting a gathering at their house in Pacific Heights so that relatives and close friends could meet the new arrivals.

He and Eva had named their daughter Millicent Audrey, after their two mothers. She'd been born four days ago with a shock of dark hair and midnight eyes.

Griffin looked across the living room to where Eva stood cradling Andrew Marcus, who'd been born two minutes before his twin. Like his sister, he was named after his grandparents. But unlike Millicent, Drew had just a stubble of dark hair and dark blue eyes whose ultimate color was anyone's guess.

Griffin thought back over the long path to today. Ultimately Eva had required a myomectomy to treat her fibroids, and they'd been unsure of the long-term results of the surgery.

He and Eva had been overjoyed to discover, after two years of marriage, that she was carrying twins.

Griffin felt a hand clap him on the shoulder, and turned to see that Marcus had come to stand beside him.

The older man held an unlit cigar in one hand and looked as if he was enjoying the prop mightily.

"It's a pink *and* blue cigar kind of day," Marcus said heartily, pointing to the two different color bands around the cigar.

Griffin looked down at his daughter, whose eyes remained closed but who blew a bubble fitfully. "Don't worry. Millicent here is taking care of blowing rings for you."

Just then, Eva walked up to them, rocking and cooing to Drew.

"I never thought I'd see the day," Marcus remarked.

"That you'd see grandchildren?" Eva guessed.

Marcus waved his cigar. "No, I mean the day you and Griffin became parents *together.* I knew you were meant for each other."

Eva lifted her brows. "Yes, your scheming saw to that, didn't it?"

Griffin suppressed a smile. Marcus had come clean—sort of—about misleading Eva into thinking Griffin had accepted a stake in Tremont REH in exchange for marrying her. Eva's father had conceded his words *could* have been subject to misinterpretation.

"It all turned out for the best, didn't it?" Marcus countered, a twinkle in his eye. "Can't argue with results, my girl."

Eva rolled her eyes. "That's just like you, to think the end justifies the means. But don't worry, I *didn't* offer Griffin ownership in Occasions by Design on the condition that he take you on as a father-in-law."

Griffin unsuccessfully stifled a laugh.

"Quick with the barb, just like your father," Marcus grumbled, though it was clear nothing could dampen his jovial mood. "Still, unlike me, you don't need Griffin to help you with your business."

Eva smiled, and a moment of connection seemed to pass between father and daughter.

Teasing and the occasional verbal sparring aside, Griffin knew a deep bond existed between father and daughter. Eva had forgiven Marcus for interfering in her life for a *second* time with his purposely misleading remarks about bribing Griffin to marry her. And now the issue of Tremont REH was also no longer such a touchy subject.

Eva had realized both her father and her husband respected her choice of career and her business judgment. Though, these days, she had delegated a lot of responsibility at Occasions by Design so she could take a maternity leave and spend time with her children.

As Eva and Marcus continued to talk, Griffin reflected on the fact that he had everything he wanted.

After his siblings had grown, he'd spent years thinking that the last thing he needed was more personal commitments and responsibilities. In retrospect, he realized it was because he took his responsibilities so seriously that he'd avoided any more of them.

But ultimately, instead of feeling free of obligations, he'd felt unconnected. He'd been adrift until he'd opened himself up to Eva.

He'd also found himself looking forward to becoming a father more than he'd thought possible. It was as if the wait—and the struggle—to conceive had just cemented his determination about what he wanted out of his life.

Eva. Kids. A home life that had been shattered with a plane crash, and that he'd spent years devoted to recreating for his siblings.

"Why are you smiling?" Eva asked.

He looked over at her. "It's impossible not to smile."

Eva couldn't agree more. If someone had said to her three years ago that she'd find herself married to Griffin Slater and the mother of twins, she'd have laughed.

Griffin's ties to Tremont REH and her father had prevented her from seeing him for what he was: husband material. Instead she'd embarked on a futile path with Mr. Wrong.

She and Griffin would celebrate their third wedding anniversary next month. And despite the stresses of her surgery and attempts to get pregnant during the first years of their marriage, they'd grown closer.

In retrospect, she was grateful for the time they'd had to forge their identity as a couple. Especially now that they'd *doubled* the size of their family in an instant—and were open to the possibility of adopting children in the future.

She looked up at Griffin. "Promise me something?"

"What?"

"Don't ever stop loving me."

He bent down for a kiss, leaning over the babies in their arms, and murmured against her lips, "You can bet on it."

* * * * *

HARLEQUIN®

INTRIGUE

WHITEHORSE MONTANA

No matter how much Nate Dempsey's past haunted
him, McKenna Bailey couldn't keep him off her mind.
He'd returned to town to bury his troubled youth—
but she wouldn't stop pursuing him until he was
working on the ranch by her side.

Look for

MATCHMAKING
WITH A
MISSION

BY

B.J. DANIELS

*Available in April
wherever books are sold.*

HARLEQUIN® Romance®

presents

The Wedding Planners

Planning perfect weddings...
finding happy endings!

Amidst the rustle of satins and silks, the scent of red roses and white lilies and the excited chatter of brides-to-be, six friends from Boston are The Wedding Belles—they make other people's wedding dreams come true....

But are they always the wedding planner...never the bride?

Who will be the next to say "I do"?

In April: Shirley Jump, *Sweetheart Lost and Found*
In May: Myrna Mackenzie, *The Heir's Convenient Wife*
In June: Melissa McClone, *S.O.S. Marry Me*
In July: Linda Goodnight, *Winning the Single Mom's Heart*
In August: Susan Meier, *Millionaire Dad, Nanny Needed!*
In September: Melissa James, *The Bridegroom's Secret*

*And don't miss the exciting wedding-planner tips and
author reminiscences that accompany each book!*

www.eHarlequin.com   HR17507

REQUEST YOUR FREE BOOKS!

2 FREE NOVELS PLUS 2 FREE GIFTS!

Silhouette®

Desire®

Passionate, Powerful, Provocative!

YES! Please send me 2 FREE Silhouette Desire® novels and my 2 FREE gifts (gifts are worth about $10). After receiving them, if I don't wish to receive any more books, I can return the shipping statement marked "cancel". If I don't cancel, I will receive 6 brand-new novels every month and be billed just $4.05 per book in the U.S. or $4.74 per book in Canada, plus 25¢ shipping and handling per book and applicable taxes, if any*. That's a savings of almost 15% off the cover price! I understand that accepting the 2 free books and gifts places me under no obligation to buy anything. I can always return a shipment and cancel at any time. Even if I never buy another book, the two free books and gifts are mine to keep forever.

225 SDN ERVX   326 SDN ERVM

Name	(PLEASE PRINT)
Address	Apt. #
City	State/Prov. Zip/Postal Code

Signature (if under 18, a parent or guardian must sign)

Mail to the **Silhouette Reader Service:**
IN U.S.A.: P.O. Box 1867, Buffalo, NY 14240-1867
IN CANADA: P.O. Box 609, Fort Erie, Ontario L2A 5X3

Not valid to current subscribers of Silhouette Desire books.

Want to try two free books from another line?
Call 1-800-873-8635 or visit www.morefreebooks.com.

* Terms and prices subject to change without notice. N.Y. residents add applicable sales tax. Canadian residents will be charged applicable provincial taxes and GST. This offer is limited to one order per household. All orders subject to approval. Credit or debit balances in a customer's account(s) may be offset by any other outstanding balance owed by or to the customer. Please allow 4 to 6 weeks for delivery. Offer available while quantities last.

Your Privacy: Silhouette Books is committed to protecting your privacy. Our Privacy Policy is available online at www.eHarlequin.com or upon request from the Reader Service. From time to time we make our lists of customers available to reputable third parties who may have a product or service of interest to you. If you would prefer we not share your name and address, please check here. ☐

SDES08

Silhouette®

SPECIAL EDITION™

Introducing a brand-new miniseries

Men of Mercy Medical

Gabe Thorne moved to Las Vegas to open a
new branch of his booming construction
business—and escape from a recent tragedy.
But when his teenage sister showed up pregnant
on his doorstep, he really had his hands full.
Luckily, in turning to Dr. Rebecca Hamilton for
the medical care his sister needed, he found
a cure for himself....

Starting with

THE MILLIONAIRE AND THE M.D.

by *TERESA SOUTHWICK,*

available in April wherever books are sold.

COMING NEXT MONTH